FLEEING WITH THE FORBIDDEN

SUBMITTING TO MY STEPBROTHER
BOOK 6

M. FRANCIS HASTINGS

CONTENTS

ONE

IBRAHIM

Will

The man himself was sitting in front of me, something I never expected to happen. Ibrahim Abadi, the sheik's most trusted minion.

"We need to get out of here," I said to McKenzie. "Immediately. Now." I grabbed her arm.

Xavier moved to block the door, but I was a fit guy, and he wasn't. I knew I could take him.

Then I heard the distinctive click of a gun being cocked. "I'd really rather you stay," Ibrahim intoned, cool as a cucumber.

"Fuck." I didn't know where to stand to best protect McKenzie as Xavier had pulled out a gun as well.

Ibrahim gestured to the seats in front of him. "Sit."

His gun didn't waver. I slid my hand down McKenzie's arm until I was holding her hand.

"I don't like this," she whispered as we trudged over to the chairs and sat down.

"I don't, either," I confirmed.

Ibrahim set the gun down on the table next to his right hand, definitely within easy reach, and steepled his fingers in front of him.

"You two are particularly difficult to catch. Almost as bad as your parents." He looked at McKenzie. "They are particularly bothersome."

"Good," McKenzie said.

Ibrahim smirked. "I can already tell you're a spitfire. Just like your parents. Especially your father. Your father is a very large thorn in my side."

I squeezed McKenzie's hand. I hoped she would take this as a signal not to antagonize Ibrahim too much. If anyone was going to draw his wrath, it was going to be me.

McKenzie did not take the hint. "I'm glad my parents are a pain in your ass. You can sit right on it and spin."

Ibrahim's lips pressed into a thin line. "You're certainly more mouthy than your mother."

"Yes, well, I've got some of my dad in the mix, too, and I know he'd tell you to go f—"

"What do you want?" I interrupted before bickering turned into hostilities. He still had the gun, after all.

Ibrahim gave McKenzie one last disapproving scowl before turning to me. "I'm glad you asked, William. I'm sure you're aware that my employer died suddenly, recently, and I've taken over his empire."

"How nice for you. Did you shoot him in the back or the front?" I asked blandly. Anything to focus his anger on me instead of McKenzie.

"Does it really matter?" He smirked, answering one of my questions. "The point is, he's dead, and I'm in charge. Now, Masterson and the sheik have been competitors in the business for many years. But there was always a mutual respect, a respect I continue to uphold with your grandfather. Imagine my surprise when he told me you had disappeared, absconding with sensitive information."

I shrugged. "Not doing me a lot of good these days, but when we *do* find a judge who isn't crooked—" I raised a derisive eyebrow at

Xavier. "—I fully intend to ram everything I know up yours and Grandfather's asses. Especially Grandfather's."

Ibrahim chuckled. "I guess someone is still a little salty over his father's suicide. That happened before you were even born. You should get over it. He was weak."

A grinding sound filled my ears, and I realized I was clenching my jaw so hard my teeth were screaming in protest. "Say that again."

He spun the gun as though we were playing Russian roulette. "Are you sure you want to play this game?"

The gun stopped spinning when the barrel was pointed right at McKenzie.

My anger was doused by panic. "Leave her out of this. She doesn't know anything."

"I very much doubt that," he chuckled. He tapped the butt of the gun near the trigger.

Next to me, McKenzie swallowed. Her hand went clammy in mine.

"Don't you need her as bait? You're trying to get Jacey and Caleb Kent, aren't you?" I pointed out.

"Killeen. But, yes." He kept tapping the gun. "Still, another Killeen is another liability. Your grandfather requested I keep you alive, but he didn't say anything about McKenzie here."

"You can tell my grandfather I have no intention of taking over the family business." I gripped McKenzie's hand. "And if you're shooting her, then you're shooting me, too."

He snickered. "I like that you think you have a choice in the matter." He picked up the gun and raised it in McKenzie's direction.

I lunged.

Ibrahim grunted in surprise, and McKenzie screamed when the gun went off.

The bullet ripped through my shoulder, and I groaned but still tried to wrest the weapon away from him.

"Enough!" he bellowed as we grappled, slamming his fist into my wounded shoulder.

I saw stars, and my hold on the gun slipped.

"Xavier," Ibrahim tsked as he got the gun away from me. "Enough child's play. Do what you were paid to do."

"McKenzie..." I murmured in defeat, just before I felt a prick in the back of my neck.

The last thing I heard was McKenzie shouting, "Will!"

<hr>

THE AIR SMELLED like hot sand and antiseptic. My shoulder was stiff but no longer burning. I was laying somewhere soft and clean.

"McKenzie," I groaned through parched lips.

A stirring of a weight on my thigh made my eyes fly open. The dry air and sudden light made them sting.

Blonde hair fanned in a cloud on top of the thin hospital blanket tucked around my body. It was McKenzie, and she was asleep.

I reached down with my good arm and stroked the back of her head, reassuring myself that she was really there.

"You're awake," a female voice said.

I looked up and saw a woman in a hijab smiling down at me. Shoulder or no shoulder, I heaved myself up to confront her or anyone else who might be with her. "Who are you?"

"I'm Dr. Rafiq's nurse, Maryam. We've been taking care of you for the past few days, though Mr. Abadi does come in from time to time," Maryam replied.

"How nice of him." I frowned. "Where are we?"

"I'm not supposed to tell you that, sorry. Mr. Abadi thinks you'll cause trouble," she chuckled.

"You do realize we've been kidnapped, right?" I said.

Maryam nodded. "Of course. But that's no reason not to be nice to you. Though you really shouldn't play with guns."

"I'll keep that in mind," I snorted.

McKenzie stirred again in my lap then sat up, blinking. "Will!" She threw herself at me.

I caught her with a grunt. My shoulder wasn't happy about her landing on my chest, but I honestly didn't give a flying fuck. She was here. She was alive. And she...

... was wearing something so gauzy it left nothing to the imagination.

I didn't even know where to put my hands to shield her from view when the doctor came in, white coat and all. "Don't move," I told her, deciding to keep her lying on my chest and gently putting my hands on her ass.

The doctor raised an eyebrow at me. "You certainly don't think *I* dressed her that way, do you?"

"No. But unless McKenzie consents, she doesn't get to be your eye candy, either," I growled.

Dr. Rafiq just rolled his eyes. "I'm perfectly happy with my wife, thank you very much." He smiled besottedly at Maryam.

"I see." I still wasn't going to let him ogle, though.

"That outfit is for *my* pleasure." Ibrahim walked in, smirking.

McKenzie stiffened in my arms.

"Didn't we have a deal, McKenzie?" Ibrahim said.

"I'm sorry," she whispered in my ear, then wriggled off me and faced Ibrahim, her cheek flushed with shame, though there was still defiance in her eyes.

I could hear something snap in my brain. I was off the bed, setting off all sorts of sensors and machines and yanking my IV right out. I grabbed McKenzie and put her behind me. "Look you sick fuck. You get her some real clothes. I don't know what kind of deal you had, but I'm breaking it."

He sighed. "You really know how to kill the mood. I was just looking. It's the least she could do for me after I provided you such excellent medical care."

"My grandfather wants me alive, so you would have had to provide me medical care anyway, you manipulative sonofabitch." I felt gauzy fabric against my back and realized I was in an open-backed hospital gown and McKenzie was trying to do the same for me as I was doing for her.

"Then it's her own fault for being stupid, isn't it?" he grinned.

McKenzie made an angry noise, but I kept her where she was by holding her arms, which she had wrapped around me.

"Clothes," I demanded again. "Now."

Ibrahim snapped his fingers, and within five minutes our old clothes, freshly-laundered, were retrieved by a servant.

My shirt had been replaced, however, with an exact copy. Unless someone's seamstress skills were so deft that the bullet hole had disappeared.

I wasn't going to worry about it. "And somewhere to change?" I continued, frowning at Ibrahim.

"Follow me." He turned and started for the infirmary door.

I threaded my fingers through McKenzie's over my stomach, and we awkwardly followed, me protecting her front, her protecting my back. The hallways dragged on forever. We were in some sort of hacienda-style building with great Moorish arches and pillars and a large garden in the middle. It was quite the compound, and I would have called it beautiful except for the fact that we were prisoners here.

"In here. I'll be locking you in, of course, and guards are posted everywhere. These will be your quarters for the time being." Ibrahim pushed open a heavy wooden door to reveal a light-filled suite with opulent furnishings. "It has an ensuite bathroom. My predecessor would have demanded you take your meals with him, however, I'm not keen on having to waste my men's time guarding you as you dart around like little mice trying to find some nook or cranny to crawl out of. I know even if I assure you there is no way out of here, you are still going to try. And I find that simply tedious."

I snatched our clothes. "Noted. I won't promise we won't try to escape, regardless."

He snorted. "I'd have been quite disappointed if you just rolled over and gave up." He winked at McKenzie, and even though I respected the fact she could defend herself, my blood still boiled.

Case in point, my brave girl spat in his face.

Ibrahim calmly took a handkerchief out of his pocket and wiped his cheek. "William Masterson III, you are quite a lucky man."

"I know." I maneuvered her and me into the bedroom and slammed the door in his face. Then I tossed the clothes down on the canopy bed and turned in her arms so I could hug her properly.

She buried her face in my chest, taking several deep breaths. I nuzzled into her hair, also taking several bracing breaths.

Then her cool fingers began to undo the ties at the back of my hospital gown.

"You want to get dressed?" I assumed, mumbling into her hair. "Probably a good idea." Still, I didn't let go.

"Actually," she replied. "I really don't."

I glanced down and tilted her chin up so I could get a good look at her. McKenzie's cheeks were flushed, her lips parted.

The way she looked up at me demurely through her lashes sent a bolt of desire straight to my groin.

"McKenzie..." I whispered, rubbing my thumb along her lower lip, "what's gotten into you?"

"Well, hopefully you in a few minutes," she replied throatily. She bit her juicy lip, and I was jealous. I wanted to be the one doing that.

Still, I had to at least *try* to be the voice of reason. I was several years older than her after all. "We're in the middle of the lion's den. Are you... sure?"

"I thought you might die," she replied, the last word choked out. "I was so scared. You were bleeding so much. And then you didn't wake up for days."

"I'm sorry, honeybee. If I could have come back to you sooner, I would have." I caressed her cheek.

"I know." She kissed my palm, and my heart melted.

Her fingers swiftly undid the rest of the ties. I let the gown slip down my arms and onto the floor before frowning at the getup

Ibrahim had put her in. It was even more see-through than I'd originally observed.

"I won't be wearing it again. *Ever*," she said in disgust.

"No. You won't. I'm going to make sure of that," I decided and gripped the offending outfit at the collar, ripping it all the way down.

TWO
HIS HONEYBEE

McKenzie

Warm, dry air wafted over my chest in the wake of Will's violent tearing of my clothes. The gauzy, ruined fabric hit the floor, leaving me in nothing but my lacy panties in front of him.

The way he was looking at them made me sure they would be his next victim.

His rage was palpable. It was hot but also a little bit scary. I put a hand on his chest, and he looked up from my panties, his blue eyes flashing and a bit unfocused in his anger. Still, he stopped and looked at me, and I took that as a good sign.

"I'm yours. You know that, right?" I said softly, rubbing a soothing circle over his heart.

Will's nostrils flared. This was a side of him I'd never seen before. Dark. Primal. Had this part of him always existed, and I just hadn't seen it under his other, more gentle layers?

His strong hand grasped the back of my neck and yanked me into a crushing kiss.

My knees went weak, and I clung to his shoulders as our bodies pressed together, his already leaking erect cock folding up between us.

We broke apart only when neither of us could breathe. Will pressed his forehead to mine and took several deep breaths. "I'm sorry. I just...."

I didn't care about what he 'just.' He just lost control. He just couldn't stand Ibrahim looking at me in a way only *he* had a right to. There were any number of 'justs.' None of them mattered now. I fused my lips to his again and swallowed the end of the sentence.

He groaned and lifted me, depositing me on the bed.

I spread my legs, trusting he was going to do exactly what he'd intended to before.

Sure enough, Will ripped my panties right off, tossing the shreds aside.

"I want you," I whispered, stroking his cheek.

He took my hand, threading his fingers through mine, and kept holding it while he prowled down my body. As if I wasn't wet enough already!

"Will," I whimpered as his lips brushed against my core.

He responded by spearing me with his tongue.

I swear if my eyes rolled back any further they would have bounced right out of my head. "Will! Oh God. Y-you don't have to. I'm already so—"

He didn't stop. He didn't care. He was ravenous. Merciless.

I tangled my fingers in his hair, too far gone now to do anything but press him to me and beg him not to stop.

Will squeezed the hand he was holding, and I knew he wasn't going to let me down. He never had, and I was sure he never would.

When I came, it was a toe-curling, star-bursting, hip-bucking experience. That he lapped up what I gave him just made it hotter.

I was so going to blow him later.

Right now, however, we both had other things on our mind. He sat up, licked his lips, then moved to hover over me even while I was still trembling in the aftermath of my orgasm.

"If you say no now, I might die, but I still have to ask," he murmured in my ear.

I grabbed his chin and forced him to look at me. "If you don't fuck me now," I growled, "*I* might die."

Will chuckled. "Yes, ma'am." He hitched one of my legs over his shoulder, widening me more for him. God knew he was going to need the space.

Holding my breath, I waited for the press of his long, thick dick. Taking him in was always a herculean effort, but I was ready.

He kissed me. "Honeybee, is it okay if I'm a little rough? I feel like I'm going crazy and that man has really pissed me off. I don't mean to take it out on you—"

"It's fine," I replied after a beat, a thrill of anticipation and trepidation going through me. "Just... for fuck's sake, Will, ravage me already!"

"Tell me if I need to stop," he replied with a sharp nod. Then he thrust. Hard.

My body barely had time to register the full length and girth of him before he pulled back and rammed in again. And again. And again. Harder and faster.

I was going to be *so* sore when this was over.

When he bit my nipple, I jumped. "Will!" I protested.

He licked the spot, and I could have come from the sore, tingling sensation. Who knew I'd like it? It sure shocked the hell out of me how my body was responding to his rough treatment.

"Is it okay?" he panted, kissing me again, all the while drilling me like a jackhammer.

"Uh-huh," I managed, yipping when he bit my other nipple.

His tongue was soft and rough at the same time, and I moaned so loud Ibrahim could probably hear me. I clapped my hands over my mouth.

"Fuck him," Will grunted, his hips slamming against mine. "Let him be jealous. You make all the noise you want, honeybee." He squeezed my hand, which was still joined with his.

"Mfph!" I kept my hands over my mouth as the tremors began, my body right on the edge of what I was sure was going to be a mind-blowing orgasm.

Just as I tipped over the edge, he yanked my hands away from my mouth. I helplessly screamed out my pleasure while he bit down hard on my shoulder, releasing into me with a rumbling groan.

He didn't pull out. Not even a bit. He stayed buried in me, still hard, as we both twitched and panted in the aftermath of the rough sex.

When I was able to catch my breath, I swatted his shoulder. "Asshole!"

Will, who had been nuzzling the mark he'd made on my shoulder, looked up. "I thought you liked it," he said, sounding concerned.

"Of course I liked it!" I snapped. "But I didn't want to let the whole house know when I came!" I swatted him again.

"I wanted to hear you, honeybee," he replied defensively. He kissed my neck. "I always want to hear you come."

"Don't be cute. I'm still mad at you," I grumped. "I didn't want *him* to hear."

He frowned. "I don't want *him* to dictate our sex life."

I pursed my lips. He had a point. "I can feel you're going to want to fuck again. Honestly, you've got more stamina than anyone I've ever heard of. This sort of thing only happens in romance novels!"

Will gave me a cheeky grin. "Aren't you a lucky girl? I'm always glad that you can keep up with me."

"Mhm. I just want you to know if you ever, *ever*, want to get lucky again, you're going to have to apologize to me and respect my wishes next time." I sniffed.

"Okay. I'm sorry. I shouldn't have let everyone in the complex hear you scream in pleasure," he responded, his blue eyes wide and innocent. The corner of his lip twitched.

"You totally don't mean a word of that." I grumbled. "But I'll take it because I want you to fuck me senseless."

"That I can do sincerely." He chuckled.

I went to hit him again, but he caught my hand and kissed it, one fingertip at a time. My cheeks heated up at the intimate gesture. Well, not just my cheeks....

Will caught on immediately. He kissed me on the lips and began thrusting, gently this time.

My body ached both from the rough sex we'd just had and with hunger for the sex we were having now. I wrapped my arms around his neck and my legs around his waist and rubbed my breasts wantonly against his chest while he slowly rode me.

"Ah, honeybee, you feel so good." He sighed, kissing me and stroking my hair. "I want to stay in you forever."

"I'd be on board with that," I agreed. My breath caught, and I knew I was going to come again, my body too overstimulated to hold back another second.

He could feel it; I knew it from his grin. He reached down between us and helped me along by massaging my clit.

Then I was coming, my core clenching around his cock as my back arched, and I shook with pleasure that exploded through every part of my body.

Will covered my lips with his and took my scream in his mouth rather than letting me alert the whole house that I was having sex and enjoying the hell out of it. I was both grateful and disappointed since this time I might not have minded. Like Will said, these people shouldn't be able to dictate our sex life.

He came inside me, letting out his moan into my mouth. I held my breath, wondering if his erection would go down this time or if we were going to be going at it like rabbits all afternoon. The idea had its appeal, true, but I was still all achy from the rough sex. I needed a break.

Then again....

When he didn't lose his erection inside me, I stroked his cheek. "Want me to blow you?" I asked, thinking about my earlier mental promise.

Will's cheeks flushed. "Sorry. I know you must be tired...."

"I'm fine. Mostly. I think my happy place needs a little break, though. So... blowjob?" I repeated.

"I swear you're a miracle," he said, finally pulling out.

My insides were both relieved and sad to feel him go. I sighed as he sat back on the bed, then got on all fours and took a firm hold of his straining cock.

He gasped, then groaned, grabbing my wrist. "I want your mouth on me. Now."

Smiling, I eagerly complied, pressing my lips over his tip, licking a drop of precum away, then taking him as deep in my mouth as I could.

"Fuuuuuuuck," he hissed. He knotted his fingers in my hair, twisting almost painfully, pushing his dick deeper down my throat.

I squeezed his thigh in warning, and he eased up.

"Sorry," he mumbled.

I patted his thigh in understanding as I began sucking him off, using my tongue and lips liberally to give him pleasure.

Since I couldn't get all of his cock down my throat, I pumped my fist up and down the exposed part of his shaft.

Will made a strangled noise. "Fuck me, honeybee."

I let go of his cock with a small pop. "Already did." I smirked, my voice a little raspy from screaming and having his cock down my throat.

"Don't stop!" he objected, trying to tug me back down by my hair.

I squeezed his shaft, and his eyes bulged. "Be nice. Honeybee's in charge now."

He nodded vigorously in understanding.

With a coy smile I leaned down and took him in my mouth again and began blowing him without mercy.

His hips bucked, and he made little desperate noises that just fueled my desire to tease him some more.

Then his breath caught, and his fingers pressed hard against my scalp. "Honeybee, I'm going to cum."

I rubbed his thigh, acknowledging his statement and giving him permission to go right ahead.

With a loud groan, he jetted his warm cum down my throat.

I swallowed, not letting him go until he'd completely finished.

Will pulled out of my mouth then pulled me up and laid down with my cheek pillowed on his chest. Looking down his body, I could see his erection had finally gone down.

"Don't do that," he said.

"Don't do what?" I asked, bewildered.

"Don't stare at it. Otherwise, it's going to get *very* happy to see you," he explained.

I giggled. I couldn't help it. "Will," I said, draping an arm over his midsection. "Give me a couple of hours to nap and then it can be just as happy to see me as it wants."

He groaned. "Promise?"

"Pinky swear," I teased.

We locked pinkies. Then we both began drifting off to sleep.

It was almost possible to forget we were in the clutches of a very bad man.

Almost.

THREE
MY WHAT?

Will

When I opened my eyes hours later, the sun was setting, casting a pinkish hue through the entrance to the small balcony and across the tile floor. The wind gently blew the curtains. If this were a honeymoon destination, it would have been perfect.

But this was no honeymoon.

I sighed. *Way to go, Will. Let's just forget where we are and fuck the stuffing out of my....* I paused. My what?

Looking down, I saw McKenzie still lying on my chest, her gorgeous, thick honey hair feathered out over her back. Her arm was still draped across my abs, her luscious breasts....

My throat went dry, and I got hard. I squeezed my eyes shut, ignoring it. I could never ignore her, however. Not in a million years.

My what? my brain prompted again.

Funny, I hadn't felt the need to define it until this moment. Did I really need to define it? We were certainly a lot more than 'friends with benefits' or 'fuckbuddies.' Just thinking those terms with regard to McKenzie disgusted me. I also couldn't quite say we were dating.

We'd never had that conversation, and, given our current situation, it wasn't exactly high on the priority list.

For some reason, the danger we were in didn't make my brain any less prone to speculation. As though this was the most important question ever asked, and even if Ibrahim decided to throw us both into the desert to die, I needed the answer more than I would need water or food.

After all, we weren't going to be on the run forever. Someday, we'd be able to stop.

Then would we stop?

I'd never thought of myself as a primal, possessive guy, but the very idea of going back to my life without McKenzie made me want to growl and beat my chest like Tarzan.

Yeah. A lot more than 'friends with benefits.' And even though we'd never discussed it, I wasn't even sure 'dating' was a strong enough word.

My what? my brain taunted me again.

I looked down again and softly stroked her silky hair. "Honeybee," I answered aloud. It was the only answer I could give.

McKenzie made cute little sounds of displeasure, clearly not wanting to wake up. She rubbed her cheek against my chest, right over my nipple, and cuddled closer, sliding her leg between mine, her thigh brushing my erection.

I let out a hiss.

"Mfph." She opened her eyes, giving me a very disgruntled look. "Is there a reason I'm awake?"

"You started it." I moved my hips so my cock rubbed against her thigh. "There's snuggling and then there's—"

She smacked her hand over my mouth, her cheeks flaming.

I grinned against her skin and licked her palm.

With a yelp, she pulled her hand back. "Will!"

"Mhm?" I rolled her beneath me, my tip poised at her entrance.

McKenzie winced.

I pulled back immediately. "Honeybee, what's wrong?"

She bit her lip. "I'm sorry. I'm really sore."

"Oh. Right. No, I'm the one who's sorry." I stroked her hair away from her face and cupped her cheek. "It's my fault."

"It was fun, though!" she said quickly. She closed the distance between us and kissed me. "I liked it. I promise. I would have said something if I didn't."

"I know. I still feel bad for hurting you." I wrapped my arms around her and sat us up so she was in my lap, and I could hug her. The fact that I'd done something to cause my honeybee pain made my dick completely deflate.

"I would have given you a hand job at least," she murmured against my lips.

I laughed. "And it would have felt fantastic, but I don't think that little horndog deserves it."

"Little? What are you calling 'little'? Have you *seen* your thing?!" she argued.

"Okay, not little. But naughty. He needs a timeout." I kissed her nose.

She snorted. "If he wasn't naughty sometimes, we'd never have any fun."

My laugh got louder, rolling out from deep in my chest. I kissed her again, slowly this time. "I—"

The scraping sound of the bolt on our door drawing back silenced whatever else I was about to say. I ripped back the covers and tossed her under them just as the door opened.

Ibrahim walked right in without so much as a 'by your leave.' "Oh good, you're awake," he said casually, as though we weren't both stark naked.

Well, I was stark naked. She'd yanked the covers up just as the door opened so only her head and bare shoulders were visible.

It was still more of her than that asshole deserved to see.

I folded my arms, just as casual as him even though I was sitting on top of the covers without a stitch on me. "You know, most people knock."

"I'm not most people," Ibrahim countered. "I see we should probably have the bedding laundered."

"You're here about semen stains?" I asked, raising an eyebrow.

He laughed. "Hardly. I'm here because your grandfather has negotiated for your transfer back to the States. Or, rather, back to his estate, where he can keep an eye on you."

A fist of panic tightened around my heart. I looked at McKenzie. "What about her?" I asked.

"I'm sure I can find a use for her until her parents are found," he replied with a lascivious smile.

It was official. I was going to kill this man someday. "That is unacceptable," I said flatly.

"I don't remember asking you. I think you'll find this is between Miss Killeen and me." He winked at McKenzie. "Nice you're already naked."

"Try it. I dare you. I'll bite it right off and shove it up your—" she began, though her hands gripped the sheets so hard they trembled.

That was it. No one was going to scare and threaten to rape my fierce little honeybee. The businessman in me told me I needed to negotiate—now. The man McKenzie held in the palm of her hand?

His arm shot out and he grabbed the startled Ibrahim by the throat.

She gasped. He gurgled.

The door slammed against the wall as a security guard kicked it all the way open. Soon, five handguns were pointed right at me.

I didn't give a flying fuck. I just kept squeezing.

"Will?" McKenzie put her hand on my arm, the other holding the sheets against her chest. "Don't kill him, Will. They'll kill you. They'll kill us both."

It took a few beats for my brain to catch up, but I finally released him.

He stumbled back, clutching his already bruising throat. "You sonofabitch," he croaked.

"And don't you forget it." I growled.

McKenzie pressed herself against my back, wrapping her free arm around my waist and laying her cheek on my shoulder blade. "It's okay, Will. Just breathe. It'll be okay."

Ibrahim scowled at me, but I knew he couldn't do shit. My grandfather wanted me. My grandfather was going to get me. I was sure it had been quite costly to William Masterson, Sr. to arrange my return, and Ibrahim didn't want to lose his down payment on a small country. Or maybe a large country. It was hard to say what sort of deal he'd managed to swing with my grandfather.

I just raised my eyebrow, daring him to retaliate.

Instead, he looked past me to McKenzie. "I owe you my life," he said with great gravity.

"Um... then if we could take the whole rape thing off the table..." she began.

He shook his head, and I was just about to change my mind about strangling him and going out in a blaze of gunfire when he continued, "I will accept Masterson's offer and send you with Will here. He didn't want you *quite* as badly, but it's a respectable sum. It doesn't really matter who has custody of you, anyway. Him, me —it's all the same. Your parents will fall on their swords to free you."

"Don't count on it," McKenzie muttered. "Dad for sure will know better than that. Them showing up isn't going to guarantee anyone's freedom."

"We'll see. I think you underestimate the sad desperation of a parent's love." He waved at his guards to leave. They finally holstered their weapons but seemed reluctant to go.

Ibrahim rolled his eyes. "I'm following you out. You two get dressed unless you want to get on the jet naked."

"My jet or yours?" I asked.

"Yours. By the time we get to the airport, it will have landed." He gave me a hateful glare that I returned steadily.

"If you two don't mind, I'd like to get dressed," McKenzie grumbled against my skin.

"Of course," Ibrahim and I said together then shared another glare.

"Jinx. You both owe me privacy for a shower. There's time for a shower, right?" she asked hopefully.

"A short one. Nothing... lengthy." He gave me an accusing look as though any delay would be solely my fault.

He wasn't wrong, but it was still annoying to be having that asshole speculating about what McKenzie and I did in private.

"Just a shower," the woman in question assured him.

Ibrahim nodded and followed his men out. "Thirty minutes. No longer."

I opened my mouth to say something sassy, but she squeezed my arm.

"What's gotten into you?" she asked, frowning at me. "This isn't like you. You don't provoke people. I provoke people. But you've been needling him since we first met him!"

My what? My brain took the opportunity to poke me again when I looked into McKenzie's green eyes.

I kissed her. I couldn't help myself. Then I pressed my forehead to hers. "I'm sorry, honeybee. I'll do better."

She swallowed, and her eyes shimmered. Was she trying not to cry? "I don't want him to hurt you again," she whispered. "Please stop antagonizing him."

"Okay." I tugged her into my lap and thumbed away the moisture. "Okay, I promise. I'll be good." I tipped her chin up so I could kiss her.

McKenzie kissed me back for a while, and it was blazing hot. But then she pulled back and swatted me. "Shower!"

My cock was not happy about this reminder. But I also didn't want us showing up in front of Grandfather's right-hand man disheveled and reeking of sex.

Ike fucking *Freeborn.* If he wasn't on the jet he was sure as hell going to be on the ground waiting to dispense my grandfather's justice. I at least wanted to be standing tall when he did it.

If I was very, very lucky, McKenzie and I wouldn't be separated. It was just a question of how much I was willing to give up to make that happen.

I stared at her, and a throbbing ache settled in the middle of my chest.

I was in so much trouble.

McKenzie, who had no idea what was going through my mind, scrunched her forehead. "Will, are you okay?"

I took a deep breath. It hurt. "Yeah, honeybee. I'm fine. You shower first."

"Okay." She kissed me swiftly, then dropped the sheets and hopped out of bed, darting naked into the bathroom.

My lips burned from the kiss, and my cock was deeply disappointed I hadn't pounced on her and made Ibrahim fuck off with his timeline. There were more important things than getting on a jet right now.

Like...

My what? my brain demanded again.

Everything, I decided firmly. *McKenzie is my everything.*

FOUR
WEIRDING ME OUT

McKenzie

After I showered, Will brushed right past me without a word to take his. He didn't even make eye contact.

Which was weird.

Then when he came out, he was wearing a towel around his waist. Like, being modest or some shit. As if I'd never seen every inch of what he was covering up.

Again, weird.

I was already dressed, but I wouldn't have bothered covering up in front of him. Not after everything we'd done together and been through. But now, he turned his back to me—turned his back!—while putting on his clothes.

We were going from weird to insulting. Or at least in insulting's zip code.

Something was definitely wrong. I wondered what had happened while I was in the shower.

"Hey... did Ibrahim come back and mess with you while I was showering?" I finally asked once his fly was zipped, and his shirt was tucked into place.

Will turned his head, looking confused. "No. Ibrahim didn't come back."

"So... what gives?" I asked, sitting down on the edge of the bed.

"Gives?" he echoed, his frown of confusion deepening.

I folded my arms over my chest. "Why won't you look at me?"

"I am looking at you." He rubbed the back of his neck and glanced away, though.

"Uh-huh. Right." I shook my head, as hurt and the idea of possible heartbreak washed over me. "So... is this where we rip the band-aid off?"

"Rip the—what are you talking about?" he responded.

"Oh come on. It's obvious *something* is wrong. You won't look at me. You don't want me to see you naked. You're not talking to me and avoiding my questions. Before this gets serious—okay, granted, I thought we were already serious, but that's on me—are you thinking it's better if we were more like friends?" I braced myself. I was a big girl. I could handle... whatever.

He stared at me, his jaw slack.

Yep, I knew it. Something was different between us, and it had taken less than half an hour apart to create some kind of rift that couldn't be bridged. That had to be it.

I felt like my guts were being ripped out, but I took a bracing breath. "I'd like it if we could stay friends." I looked down at my hands that I was trying not to clench in my lap. "Though, you do need to know, I don't do 'friends with b—'"

A strong hand yanked my chin up. I hadn't even heard him move. "Stop talking," he said sternly. "Just stop."

"But—"

Will's lips crushed to mine with such force and passion that all I could do was grab his shoulders to keep from falling backward. I couldn't breathe. I didn't care.

When he did pull back to let me gasp in some air, he put a finger over my lips. "No more talking nonsense. We are serious. We were never 'friends with benefits.' And no one's ripping off any band-aids."

"Oh." I felt pretty stupid but also very relieved.

"I'm sorry if I made you feel insecure in our relationship," he continued, pulling me up into a hug and nestling his stubbled chin in my hair. "Why were you so worried all of a sudden?"

Feeling even more like an idiot, I stuttered out the signs I'd picked up.

"So, in ten minutes of me 'acting weird,' you decided I wanted to end things?" he asked.

I winced. "When you put it that way... I mean... we never *officially* started things...."

He chuckled, and his arms tightened around me. "Then we're officially starting things. Now. And if that asshole wasn't coming to collect us in the next five minutes, I'd make sure we sealed that deal right here and now in the best possible way. But this will have to do." He kissed me again.

Several minutes must have passed because the rap of knuckles on wood finally broke us apart. Ibrahim was there in the doorway with five guards. "Let's go," he said.

We followed him out into the hall where Will put his arm around my waist, tucking me into his side while we walked. Three black SUVs were parked in the complex's courtyard. Ibrahim, Will, and I slid into the middle one.

Will took my hand as we sat hip-to-hip. As the SUVs took off, I suddenly had a thought.

"Hey," I whispered to Will. "What was up with your weird behavior?" He'd never explained himself, and I wanted to know.

He raised an eyebrow at me. "Later. I promise."

The look I gave him told him on no uncertain terms that I wasn't going to forget or let the subject drop, but I nodded my agreement when I saw Ibrahim regarding us with a slight smirk.

"It's always an intense and vulnerable moment when a man realizes what he wants." Ibrahim grinned. "Must be scary, now knowing you would do anything to keep it. Morals, righteous indignation, none of it matters anymore, does it?"

"Shut up," Will growled.

"Masterson is going to be so pleased. This couldn't have gone better if he'd planned it. He's got you *and* the Killeens by the balls because of one cute little twenty-something." Ibrahim laughed almost maniacally.

Will scowled, and I squeezed his hand. "Don't listen to him. He's just being an ass."

"I have to be one now. I'm not going to have the opportunity much longer." Ibrahim leaned back in his seat, pleased with himself. "I knew you'd realize it eventually. All the ramifications. I'm just delighted I could be here to see it."

"He's not going to compromise his morals because of me. Someone who actually *had* morals would know that," I said.

However, Will did look troubled.

I sighed angrily. "William Masterson *the Third*, you will *not* do anything unethical just because we're serious."

"Is that what they call it these days?" Ibrahim was enjoying this far too much.

I wondered what kind of maneuvering it would take to kick him in the balls from the back seat. Maybe when the car stopped.

Will slid an arm around my shoulders and tucked me into his side. "As far as I know, it's about to be none of your business what I do or what decisions I make. I think you're pawning that one off on my grandfather."

"It would still be something to see. Masterson crushing you one compromise at a time. You're not going to be so self-righteous anymore. Thinking this life is beneath you." Ibrahim tapped his chin in thought. "Maybe you'll kill yourself like your father."

My jaw dropped. Though Will tried to stop me, I reached out and yanked Ibrahim's hair so hard that a fistful came away in my hand.

Ibrahim shouted, trying to swat me but hitting the driver instead.

The SUV veered wildly.

Will reached across and snapped my seatbelt into place just before the driver was able to right our course. Straight into a tree.

I threw up my hands, screaming, "Will!"

My seatbelt grabbed me and launched me back into the seat when the force of the crash tried to fling me forward. The world around me was chaos, glass flying, Ibrahim's coffee splashing all over. The crunching noise was deafening. As were the screams.

Making sense of my surroundings proved difficult, even when it was all over. I blinked, not even remembering my own name for a second.

"... 'kenzie..." a familiar voice was saying.

A hand on my thigh brought my focus back, and, ears still ringing, I looked over at Will. Who was also, miraculously, wearing a seatbelt. I hadn't noticed.

Relief slammed into me so hard that I couldn't stop the choking tears from bursting out of me. "Will!"

He unbuckled my seatbelt and started to undo his own but I crawled into his lap before he could, ignoring the sprinkling of glass. I kissed him and touched him all over, reassuring myself that he was alive.

"I'm okay," he said, wrapping his arms around me. He was scratched up, probably from the flying glass. But as far as I could tell, he was otherwise fine.

"I'm sorry. That was stupid of me. It's all my fault. So, Ibrahim, you can blame me and—" I turned toward the front.

Will smacked a hand over my eyes. But it was too late. I'd seen there was no longer a 'front.' And there was no longer an Ibrahim. Or a driver.

"H-Holy..." I gasped.

"Let's get out of the car," he said calmly. "No doubt Ibrahim's people are coming to get us even as we speak." He ran his hands over me, then. "Are you hurt? You're all scratched up."

"So are you," I pointed out. I looked through the back window to see Ibrahim's guards coming down an embankment.

Will gently set me back on my seat, then disengaged his seatbelt. He opened his door with effort, having to put his shoulder into it, then got out and reached for me.

I went straight into his arms.

The guards brushed right past us and went to see what was left of their boss. I wasn't stupid enough to think we could just run, though, and neither was Will.

"Let's just stay put for a while," he said, and I could feel a soft tremble in his body. That was fine by me. I was shaking like a leaf.

With a disgusted grunt, the leader of the guards gathered the others together, no doubt to discuss the situation.

Will and I just stood still in each other's arms, waiting for the next shoe to drop.

Finally, all eyes turned to us.

"How much?" the guard in charge asked.

"How much what?" Will replied.

"How much will you give us to say you died in this accident?" the guard elaborated. "We can't get money from him anymore." He jerked his thumb at what was left of Ibrahim.

I was pretty sure my college financial aid wasn't going to satisfy them, and I didn't know how to access it from here anyway.

As far as I knew, Will was in pretty much the same boat, with his access to Masterson assets frozen.

"Where are we?" Will asked, surprising me. I wondered if he was playing along for time.

"Spain," the guard said.

Will nodded slowly. "How does twenty-five million sound?"

"Not as good as fifty," the guard countered.

I stared at Will. "Where are you going to get twenty-five million—?"

"Shh." Will kissed my forehead. "For once, I've got this." To the guard, he said, "Done."

The guard nodded. "We will take her as insurance. Samson will drive you wherever you need to go. We will follow."

Will frowned, clearly not liking the plan. "I don't—"

"This is a one-time offer. The terms are set. Get us the money or run off, and we'll ransom her to the highest bidder," the guard said.

"I'm not going to run off," Will argued.

"Good. Then we won't have any problems." The guard nodded to two other men.

They came forward and wrenched Will and me apart.

"McKenzie!" Will protested, reaching out, but the guard in charge smacked his hand away.

"Remember our deal. Fifty-million dollars, and you can both go free," the guard said.

Will's hands balled into fists while I struggled in our captors' vice-like grips. "If you hurt her, you'll regret it."

The guard snorted. "Brave talk for a man in your position." He turned to the others. "Move out."

FIVE

FIFTY MILLION

Will

I hoped I wasn't doing something stupid. Well, I knew I was doing something stupid. And not thought out. And dangerous. But at least I hoped it wasn't going to get us killed.

McKenzie kept giving me a *what the fuck?!* look. I didn't blame her. How could she know I'd stashed money away in a private European bank?

I almost laughed at the hubris of the twenty-something young man I had been who decided he was going to stick it to Grandfather for taking football away by starting a new life in Spain. It was also a kick in the gut about how privileged I'd been that I'd moved fifty-million dollars to a foreign country and basically forgotten about it.

Still, Spain! Of all the places we could have ended up....

McKenzie was put in a different black SUV than mine, which irked me, but they had fifty million reasons to give her back, so I decided to bide my time. They weren't going to hurt her. Or me. Money made things easy that way.

"El Banco Palacios in Madrid," I said tersely to the main guard. I frowned at him. "And I don't think I caught your name."

"You didn't. And you're not going to," the guard replied conversationally. But there was a layer of steel to his words.

"I'll call you MacDuff," I decided.

He laughed. "As in 'lead on'?"

"Yes."

MacDuff nodded. "I like it. Okay, guys, you heard the man. Let's get his rich ass to Madrid."

I glanced through the back window, but the vehicle behind us had tinted windows, just like ours. I couldn't see McKenzie, but I knew she was there.

MacDuff patted my shoulder. "Don't worry. She's just fine. If she puts up too much of a fuss, my guys will just drug her, and she can just sleep the whole way there."

I grimaced. "That's... disturbing."

"Better than her trying to do something stupid like jump out while we're speeding down the carretera," he pointed out.

I winced. "Good point."

"I knew you'd see it my way." He offered me a bottled water.

Suspicious, I took it and examined it. The seal was unbroken. "What's this for?"

"Truce. As long as we get our money, you two are off the hook. You can fly off free as birds. I mean, I can't guarantee there won't still be people coming after you, but the boss is dead, and your grandfather's back in the United States, so... I'm thinking your odds might be a little better here," he said.

I eyed the bottle, then cautiously twisted the cap off. Sniffing the water within, I finally took a sip.

"Don't trust me?" he asked.

"No," I replied, taking another cautious sip. "I don't."

"Good. You shouldn't." Then he pulled a syringe from his jacket.

"You've got to be kidding me," I growled. I went for my seat belt release.

MacDuff grabbed my wrist. "If you make me chase you around

this car, you're not going to like the consequences. Now, that nice young Killeen girl—nice going, by the way, she's hot and what, half your age?—is getting the same treatment. It's just going to make the ride a little shorter. And less stressful for the rest of us."

They want the money. They want the money. No need to make trouble. Besides, how would I get to McKenzie anyway? "I really hate you." I moved my hand away from the seat belt release and offered my arm instead. "And she's not half my age."

"Riiight." He injected me with whatever was in the syringe.

I was out in seconds.

A SLAP-SLAP-SLAPPING sound pulled me from a groggy fog. I realized, once I became aware of my cheeks stinging, that I was getting lightly slapped across the face.

"Could you stop?" I grunted, peeling my eyelids open with effort. "I'm awake."

"There he is! I think I gave you a little too much. But we're here," MacDuff said.

A little too much? My attention snapped to the vehicle parked behind us. The black SUV's windows were no less tinted than they had been before. If they'd given 'almost too much' to a grown, fit, thirty-year-old man, what would the same dose have done to McKenzie?!

"Relax. Hers was calibrated better. She's been awake for a while. Mouthy little thing, too." He chuckled as though reading my mind.

I looked out the side window at el Banco Palacios then back at him. "I'm not doing shit until I see she's okay."

He held up his hands. "Peace, my friend. I knew you were a smart man and weren't going to just give us the money without guarantees." He pulled out his phone.

"A video won't suffice," I argued.

"Of course it won't. But I do need to make sure she's calm before we go over there. Witnesses and all that. You understand," he said.

"Ah." That would be a consideration.

MacDuff barked some orders into his phone in a language I didn't understand then turned to me. "No scenes from you, either."

"No scenes," I promised.

He got out of the SUV then came around and opened my door.

I stepped out into the sun, my eyes burning at the sudden flash of light, and quickly shielded my eyes.

Very calmly, he put a hand on my back as though escorting a celebrity. The back door of the other SUV swung open, and McKenzie was sitting there, looking frazzled but intact.

I couldn't say the same for her captors. All three were sporting bites and scratches. It made me smile. "How are you doing?" I asked her calmly. I needed to make sure the situation stayed as peaceful as possible.

"They drugged me." McKenzie scowled at the three men in the SUV.

"Me, too," I responded sympathetically. I started to reach out to her, but MacDuff caught my arm.

"That's enough for now," he said. "We've got an appointment at a bank."

I swore under my breath. "Unless you did something while I was out, I didn't make an appointment."

"That kind of money? You probably don't need one." He ushered me away from McKenzie. The SUV door closed with a thunk of finality behind us.

"Lead on," MacDuff grinned, gesturing.

I crossed the busy street, congested with both vehicle and foot traffic, and walked up to the bank. I looked at the ornate metal double doors, thick enough to stop a tank, and wondered if they'd even take a guy dressed in a wind suit. I was dressed like the quintessential American tourist and certainly not like anyone with money.

Plus, there was another problem.

"I don't have my ID," I murmured to MacDuff as the doors swung wide, opened by very professional employees who, to their credit, did not bat an eyelash at my attire.

He grinned and pulled something out of his jacket pocket. "We did need to get you back to the United States. Masterson had these couriered pretty quickly."

Damned if the man wasn't holding a passport, social security card, and birth certificate for both McKenzie and me!

"I see," I said. "Not a problem, then."

"No problems here. Only solutions." He walked right up to the main desk. "Hi, we'd like to see the manager."

The woman behind the desk looked us over. "May I ask what this is concerning?"

"William Masterson the Third would like to make a withdrawal from his account," MacDuff continued smoothly.

Something in her manner should have alerted us. Or at least him. He was a trained mercenary, after all.

But then, the woman only paused for the smallest of moments before picking up her phone. "Señor Palacios, Mr. William Masterson the Third is here. He is one of our larger account holders. He is asking to see you about a withdrawal."

I couldn't hear the other side of the conversation, but the woman nodded several times, then motioned to a guard. "Please get Mr. Masterson and his friend settled," she told him.

"Mr. Masterson. Got it." The guard turned to us. "Follow me, por favor."

"Gracias," MacDuff said and followed the guard. He must have been very distracted by the idea of fifty-million dollars because even I caught sight of other bank guards peeling away from their stations and following behind us.

It made me jumpy and suspicious. I wasn't sure if I should say something to MacDuff so the two of us could try to make a run for it, or if I should let it be and let the chips fall where they may. *Devil I know? Devil I don't...?*

In the end, I decided there were too many of them. I didn't want anything to happen to McKenzie if we caused a scene. All I could do was hope and pray at this point that McKenzie and I would come out of this unscathed because I was certain now it was out of my hands.

I was not surprised at all to see Ike when they swung a door open and ushered us inside a small conference room. He was seated beside who I could only assume was the bank manager and had a bodyguard standing behind him.

"Will." Ike smiled, standing. "You're a hard man to find. Why don't you sit down? Your friend here isn't going anywhere."

"He's not my friend," I said flatly. "I'm in the middle of a business deal. Do you mind?"

"Would that be a business deal where you drain your paltry little savings here in order to buy you and your girlfriend out of trouble? No need. I'd hate for you to waste your hard-earned money on something your grandfather and I can easily do for you. How much did he offer you, Mr. Ingram?" Ike asked.

MacDuff's jaw dropped. "How did you know my—?"

"It's not really that important, is it?" Ike crossed his arms over his chest. "I just need a number and a girl, and then you're free to go."

"A hundred million," MacDuff lied, his eyes daring me to correct him.

"Oh, I very much doubt that. But let's call it a hundred-and-fifty million, and I never see you or your colleagues again," Ike replied smoothly.

"Done." MacDuff, or Mr. Ingram, or whoever he really was, pulled out his phone. "Bring the girl to—"

"The front door will do just fine," the bank manager spoke up.

MacDuff nodded. "Bring her to the front door and leave her there as soon as you see me walking out."

"Will, please, sit. You look like you've been having quite a rough time. And those clothes!" Ike grimaced.

I gritted my teeth, but sat down. "Ike..."

"You can thank me later by being nicer to your grandfather. He's been really quite worried about you." Ike cut me off. Then, he turned to MacDuff. "Let's conclude our business. I've got a jet burning fuel on the tarmac as we speak."

The bank manager brought out some paperwork and an iPad. There was some mumbling between the three of them about the details, which made the time drag on even longer. I didn't want McKenzie in Ike's hands any more than I wanted her out there with a pack of mercenaries. But I did want her with me. As soon as possible.

Finally, the bank manager signed the paperwork himself, and it was a done deal.

"McKenzie," I said gruffly when MacDuff stood.

"I'm getting her. Keep your pants on." He chuckled. He shook hands with Ike then headed out.

I turned to Ike, feeling itchy under my skin. "What are you going to do with us?"

He leaned forward, steepling his hands in front of himself, a victorious smile on his face. "I'm glad you asked, Will. I have to thank you for running off and getting yourself all twisted up over a nice young thing. Your grandfather and I weren't sure how we were going to get you back to work—how to get you to embrace your destiny. This was a lot bigger than that ridiculous football fantasy of yours, after all. I mean, I'd been prepared to have your leg broken in a mugging, but you saw sense. This time, though, you really went thermonuclear and made all the wrong choices due to some misguided sense of morality. Silly boy."

Anger erupted in me, but I tamped it down. He could call me 'boy' all he wanted to as long as he got me McKenzie. I'd already realized what my situation had become, even without him finishing his explanation.

Ike was determined to have his villain's monologue, however. Only this time, I didn't think anyone was coming to rescue us at the last second. "Now that we have McKenzie, well, things have become so much easier. Wouldn't you agree, Will? You get the love of your life. We get our figurehead back. In the public eye, all is right in the world."

"Fine." It was the only response to give, after all.

SIX

THE STATUS QUO

McKenzie

The men in the SUV suddenly yanked me out and into the street. They held up their hands to stop traffic, hustling me along as though I were an A-list celebrity. How I would have liked to tell those curious eyes watching us from all sides that I was, in fact, a hostage.

I didn't, though, because of Will. I didn't want anything bad to happen to him.

They brought me right up to the door of the bank and dumped me there, their leader practically skipping out of the bank. He winked at me. "Good luck, beautiful."

Good luck? I didn't like the sound of that. "Hey, where's W—?"

The bank doors opened, and two guards grabbed me, one on each arm.

"Hey!" I protested.

"Things will get a lot more difficult if you make a scene," one guard mumbled in highly accented English.

"Where is Will?" I hissed back, struggling less. We *were* drawing attention, I could tell by the frowns from different desks. Employees and patrons alike were watching us.

"Mr. Masterson is in a meeting. But we are bringing you there now," the guard said, exasperated. "Now please, stop fighting, Miss Killeen."

I ground my teeth but stopped making them drag me. "It's Kent."

"Whatever. Let's go." They escorted me to a very large set of heavy wooden doors. One guard produced a skeleton key—old school—and unlocked them. He pushed open the doors and nudged me inside.

Will stood and turned, and, despite all the other people in the room, I ran straight into his arms, knocking into him so hard he grunted. But he didn't seem to mind. He folded his arms around me and held me tight.

"Aw, that's adorable," a voice I didn't recognize said, and I felt the rumble of a growl in Will's chest.

"Are we in trouble again?" I asked, my voice tired and unsurprised. I already knew the answer.

"Yes," Will sighed.

I nodded against his shirt. "What's the cost?"

"My soul. Your freedom," Will replied flatly.

"Sounds about right." I kept my voice bland as well.

The new captor, because that had to be who he was, laughed at our exchange. "I'm glad you're already used to the situation. That will make this even easier. Come on, everyone. Let's get to the jet. You'll have more appropriate clothing waiting there. I wonder if I should call a stylist? Just in case the press is waiting when we land."

I didn't bother raising my head, and Will didn't let me go.

"That was more of an order than a suggestion," the man continued when we didn't move.

Will reluctantly transferred me to his side, taking my hand. "You're a real pain in the ass, Ike."

"I know," Ike replied unrepentantly. He stood, and the hulking man behind him handed him his jacket. "It will be good to have you back in the office. We could only make so many excuses for your absence."

"Gee, I'm so sorry I made things difficult for you," Will deadpanned.

"Is this a family member?" I asked Will quietly.

Will choked, looking horrified.

Ike laughed in delight. "Oh, aren't you a little angel? No, I'm more of an associate. My name is Ike Freeborn. You can call me Ike, if you like."

"Oh. The right-hand man," I said, smacking my forehead. "Of course."

"In the flesh." Ike looked up at his bodyguard. "Are the boys ready, Tom?"

"Yes, sir, Mr. Freeborn," Tom replied. "They won't be getting away this time."

"Good." Ike gestured for us to walk ahead of him. "The bank guards will escort you to the door. Then there will be another nice set of gentlemen in suits at the entrance to take you to our vehicles."

"Black SUVs?" Will inquired.

Ike laughed. "Oh, you have been through the wars, haven't you? No, black town cars. But good guess." He looked us both up and down again and sighed. "I really wish we had something more suitable to dress you in now. People will be thinking all sorts of things between here and the jet. There's no saying there aren't already reporters in Spain parked out at the tarmac."

"We match, at least." Will smiled slightly and put his arm around me.

Ike rolled his eyes. "That's half the problem."

I had to smile right along with Will. Sure, we were in a tough spot, but at least we could try to make this asshole's life a living hell.

To that end, Will kept his arm around me and was visibly affectionate, bumping his hip gently against mine and kissing my temple as we walked. My smile widened. It was nice that we were on the same page. I put my arm around his waist for good measure.

"I suppose we'll have to do an engagement announcement sooner rather than later," Ike despaired. He wanted to throw us off balance.

And I was a little thrown. I missed a step as we walked through the bank doors, but Will caught me and kissed me hard on the lips.

I melted and wrapped my arms around his neck, opening my mouth so he could deepen the kiss. Just like that, the world completely fell away.

"Oh for the love..." Ike poked me in the arm. "Let's go, you two."

Will dragged his lips from mine and fixed Ike with an icy glare. "You don't *ever* touch her."

"Yes, fine. I'm sure you have a big dick. Let's get to the plane," Ike huffed.

"I mean it," Will said, tucking me into his side again. "You don't lay one filthy finger on her ever again, or I swear I will make your life feel like the ninth tier of Hades."

Ike raised an eyebrow. "I almost want to test that. But that's for a different day." He motioned to men in suits who had been waiting patiently on the sidewalk. "Let's go."

The men formed a tight ring around Will, Ike, and me. Like Ibrahim's guards, they stopped traffic to get us to a line of three black town cars. People were now so curious, having seen me surrounded like a celebrity twice now, that they'd started taking out their phones and were filming.

I thought about screaming that we were being kidnapped. I looked up at Will.

As though he'd read my mind, he shook his head at me. "It will make things worse," he whispered.

Defeated, my shoulders slumped. "We're really going along with this, aren't we?"

"Yes," he confirmed, not sounding happy about it.

"Are we... actually going to have an engagement announce-ment?" I asked, not sure how I felt about the idea.

He paused while we settled ourselves in the back of the second town car. Ike was in the first.

"McKenzie... I didn't want anything to happen the way it's happened. And there's going to be a lot down the road that I don't want to happen the way it's going to happen," Will said slowly as the cars pulled away from the curb. "But I love you, and I want to be with you. That much I know. Engagement announcements, parties, weddings, birth announcements, christenings, I can see it all lining up like we're going through some tunnel. And Grandfather will want it all sooner rather than later." He raked a hand through his hair. "I'd have wanted to take you to Barcelona and proposed in some hidden nook in Park Güell after we'd dated for at least two years. I'd... want you to be sure. I know none of this is going to be fair, and it's all going to be rushed. I hate that for both of us. But I don't know how to stop it, or even slow it down, either."

It was a lot to take in. "So... we're getting engaged. And married. And then I'm... going to... have a baby?" I asked, trying to make sure I understood correctly. My chest was tight with panic.

"Yes," he responded, closing his eyes. "That's how Grandfather will want it. I hope."

"How else would he want it?" I swallowed.

Will looked pained. "He'd... want you to be a surrogate and carry the Masterson heir, like your mother. He'd take you away from me. I need to stay on his good side or things won't go well for either of us, but especially not for you."

I couldn't breathe. I had no idea what my face looked like, but he quickly put a hand on the back of my neck and guided my head between my knees.

"She need a sedative?" one of Ike's men asked.

Will shook his head vehemently. "No. I don't want her being knocked out again today. I don't think that's good for a person."

"It won't hurt her," the man assured him.

"No." Will's voice was firm as he massaged the back of my neck.

I wondered if it would really be a bad thing. My heart felt like it was going to pound itself right out of my chest.

"He knows I won't be his good little grandson if he does anything like that to you," Will assured me. "I think we're all just going to go through the motions. It'll be okay. I will *make* it okay."

Because I wasn't capable of anything else in that moment, I just nodded. Once I was breathing easier, Will unbuckled me and pulled me into his lap.

My mind reeled, but I was grateful for his solid presence. I wondered how my mother would feel—had felt—in a similar situation. Or my father. He certainly hadn't had the leverage Will did to keep Mom safe. Surely, my situation with Will was better?

When the cars stopped at a hangar, I realized Will hadn't said anything for a while. I looked up to find an expression on his face I'd never seen before. Stony.

"Will...?" I asked.

"Let's get on the jet," he replied. He was almost cold.

I shivered.

His arms tightened around me briefly, but he did let me go once one of Ike's men swung open the passenger door.

"Will..." I said worriedly as we walked to the jet and climbed the stairs into it. It was a nice jet, the kind you'd see in movies—new and clean and well-appointed. The cabin was also quite large. But I didn't really pay attention to all that.

"We'll be in the back," he called to Ike who came on the jet behind us.

"Of course. There's proper clothing in there. And a shower," Ike said.

"I know," Will grunted.

Ike smirked. "She doesn't."

Will tugged me into the back of the jet and opened a sliding door. A motion-sensing light went on, and I found myself staring at a large bed with a few sets of clothes laid out on it, mine on one side, his on the other.

"Will, if you're worried about me, I can handle it. I can handle it all because I'm going to be with you," I said after watching him stare off into space for too long. I touched his arm. "I love you. We can get through this together. I'll be your wife. The mother of your children. Sure, it's a lot faster than I'd like, and there are still some college and career things I'd like to do, but we can figure it out...."

"I know why he killed himself," he replied as though he hadn't heard me.

I froze. "What?"

"My dad. I could never figure out why he did it. But I know now. He didn't feel like he had any other options. He knew the people he loved were just going to get more and more hurt." He shook his head slowly. "He knew he was going to be stuck under *that man's* thumb forever."

I didn't like where this was going. "Will...."

He took a deep breath. "I wonder if it made anything easier or helped anyone else—"

I couldn't help myself. I slapped him.

Hard.

SEVEN
SLAP SOME SENSE

Will

I stumbled back, dazed, my hand going to my cheek.

McKenzie shook her hand out, grimacing. She really had slapped me hard.

"What was that for?" I asked her, frowning.

"That was so you didn't go find a razor in the bathroom and do something stupid!" she shouted. "Ouch, damn, that hurt!" She massaged her hand.

"You're telling me," I snorted, rubbing my face. Then the rest of her words caught up with me. "McKenzie, did you think I was going to kill myself?"

"You were sure making it sound like you were!" she said. She began to pace.

"I was just having a moment," I argued. I stopped her with my hands on her shoulders. "We've had this conversation before—"

"Yeah, but you didn't have that look on your face before," she replied accusingly. There were tears in her eyes.

"Oh, honeybee." My annoyance quickly dissipated, and I

dragged her into my arms. "I'm sorry. I didn't mean to scare you. I wasn't going to leave you that way. I never will. I promise."

She gave a little hiccup, and I felt like an asshole as her tears began soaking into my shirt. "I can handle it," she murmured, her nails digging into my back. "I can. I can handle anything. As long as I have you."

My heart broke and swelled at the same time. I wasn't sure how that was even possible. "Honeybee, I love you. I love you so much. Please don't cry. I won't leave you." I kissed her hair.

McKenzie raised her tear-stained face and suddenly pressed her wet lips to mine. She was desperate… and hungry.

"We shouldn't be here," I breathed against her lips even as every fiber of my being told me we should. Here. There. Everywhere.

"Why not?" she asked. "There's a perfectly good bed right there. Or we could shower. Or both."

Both! my cock insisted.

"Ike's on board. And all those bodyguards," I pointed out, trying to get the little fucker to stop shouting his opinion.

McKenzie shrugged. "When won't they be around?"

I swallowed. "Good point."

She slid her hand down to cup the troublemaker in question. "I'm getting an enthusiastic response from the man downstairs."

"The man downstairs would have to be dead not to respond to you," I replied with a chuckle. "God… honeybee, are you sure?"

In reply, she stepped back and began taking off her clothes.

I locked the pocket door then turned to find her at eye level with my dick. My throat went dry as she opened my pants. "You know, this really isn't necessary," I wheezed as she scooped out my cock and licked her lips. "He's already very riled up…."

McKenzie pressed her lips over the head of my cock, and I had to brace myself against the door. "H-Holy shit," I gasped, my fingers sinking into her hair.

Like the champ she was, McKenzie took me down her throat. She'd gotten really good at taking me with her mouth, which I knew could be no small feat. I groaned and tightened my grip on her hair while she did something sinful with her tongue.

"Honeybee," I panted after a while, "unless you want me to cum in your mouth, I suggest—oh Jesus—I suggest we move things to the—ah!—bed."

Her response was to squeeze my balls and deep-throat me as far as she could.

I couldn't help myself. I exploded, pumping my cum down her throat.

McKenzie coughed a little but managed to swallow every drop. She let my dick go with one last little lick over the tip and grinned up at me.

Oh, she knew she'd been naughty. Deliciously so.

I pulled her up by her arms, holding her against me as I devoured her clever mouth. I could still taste me on her lips.

She pulled back to catch her breath. "Did you like something I did?" she asked innocently.

"Mhm. And I'm going to like it even more when I'm deep inside you listening to you scream," I replied, my voice rumbly and full of heat.

"Oh, is that what you think is going to happen?" she teased.

"That's what I *know* is going to happen," I growled. I started undressing her while she pretended to think about it, barely suppressing her giggles.

"But what if he's tired?" she asked, reaching between us to stroke my dick.

I stiffened. At thirty, I shouldn't have been popping an erection every five minutes, but this woman drove me wild. "He's not tired," I chuckled, telling her what she was already finding out for herself.

I snapped open her bra clasp.

"Are you a boob guy?" she asked me when I dragged her bra off her and stared, mesmerized, at her chest.

"A boob guy?" I repeated with a laugh.

She shrugged, and I realized she was serious.

"McKenzie, if you're wondering right now about my former partners and my tastes with them, it's really bad timing," I said, wondering where this was coming from. I brushed her hair off her cheek and kissed her again. "But I need you to know there is only one McKenzie, and I'm a McKenzie guy. I like everything about your body, mind, and spirit. I just want to wrap you around me all the time. Do they make McKenzie security blankets?"

"I just... suddenly thought about how you're stuck with me," she responded, her cheeks flushing. She looked at the floor. "Yeah, sorry, bad timing, I know."

This absolutely needed to be nipped in the bud. Mr. Fun Times was just going to have to wait. I put my cock back in my pants and guided her, with her underwear still on, over to the bed. I took her hands as I sat her down beside me.

"McKenzie, look at me," I said.

She bit her lip. "I'm sorry. I ruined the mood."

"We'll get it back. It's not important right now," I replied. I tipped her chin up and locked eyes with her. "I need you to know that I mean every word I'm about to say. Okay?"

She swallowed and nodded.

"I. *LOVE*. You." I enunciated the words clearly. "I don't think of any other women when I'm with you. You have completely obliterated anyone who has ever come before you from my mind and my life. There is only McKenzie. I don't want anyone else. I won't ever want anyone else. You are everything to me. Everything." I took a deep breath. "But I understand. I'm worried I'm taking away your whole future. You're nineteen. There are things you deserve to experience—"

Her eyes welled up with tears, and she gripped my hands. "But I don't want any of that. Not without you."

"Honeybee, how can you possibly know that?" I asked, my own doubts showing.

"What exactly am I supposed to experience? More boys?" she argued.

I flinched. I was pretty sure if I ever saw her with another man, I'd kill him. Fuck, I might kill them both.

"That's right. That's exactly how I feel thinking about you making a future with another woman," she said. "I just... it's not like I want you to... I think it might kill me if you found somebody else... but I just... you don't have the freedom."

"And you don't, either," I pointed out.

McKenzie climbed into my lap and hugged her nearly naked body to mine. "That isn't fair to you."

I wrapped my arms around her and chuckled sadly. "Honeybee, it's not fair to *you*. But it sounds like neither of us is looking for a way out of it, either. You make me happy. I wouldn't trade you for anyone or anything else."

"Then I guess I got upset over nothing," she mumbled, running her fingers through my hair, making my scalp—and other places—tingle.

"It's never nothing to talk about our relationship. I'd rather you say something than let it fester," I said. I stroked her bare back.

She looked up, and I could see the question in her eyes.

I put my finger over her lips. "I'm not telling you my number. And you're not telling me yours."

"Why not?" she asked.

"Because the next thing I'm going to ask for is names, and then I'm going to want to personally go and rip their dicks off," I said flatly. "And don't tell me you won't feel exactly the same about mine."

"I'd only scratch their eyes out," she grinned. "God, I never thought of myself as a jealous person."

"Me, neither. But here we are. Doesn't that alone tell you we belong together?" I replied.

McKenzie nodded slowly. "Yeah, I think it might."

I laughed and rolled her underneath me. "Now that that's settled, how about we go back to what we were doing, hmm?"

She tugged my shirt over my head. "That sounds like a great idea."

I kicked off my shoes, pants, and boxers and spread her thighs. I saw her glistening and licked my lips.

McKenzie shook her head vehemently.

"What?" I asked. "You don't want me to go down on you?"

She shook her head again. "I want you inside me. Now."

My cock was thrilled by her words, but I made myself hold onto the few remaining brain cells that weren't on Team Dick. "Are you sure? I haven't even—"

McKenzie grabbed my cock, and I grunted, all my brain cells falling over dead. "If you don't put it in me now, William Masterson the Third, I swear I'm going to die!"

"Well," I purred, putting my hand over hers and, together, giving my cock a little stroke. "We can't have that." I helped her guide me to her entrance.

She arched her back as I pushed inside, and, while she was warm and wet—two things my dick was very happy about—I still wondered if I'd hurt her. There hadn't been a lot of foreplay....

I groaned as she wriggled, widening her thighs even more.

"Damn, I keep forgetting how *big* you are!" she grunted.

"Is that... a compliment or a complaint?" I managed, gasping as her nails dug into my ass and encouraged me to sink inside her all the way to the hilt.

"Who's complaining?" she giggled.

I kissed her hard and palmed her soft breast, flicking her nipple with my thumb as I started to move. "Sure as hell not me."

McKenzie wrapped her legs around my waist, biting her lip again as she raised her hips to meet my thrusts.

Seeing the hazy pleasure in her eyes started an answering pounding in my chest. It wasn't the first time I felt something primal when I was with her. I considered myself a modern man, but feeling her writhe beneath me, watching her skin flush all over, and hearing her moan my name when she came apart—made me want to mark her as MINE. So no man would ever dare to look at her, much less touch her.

She nodded as her inner muscles clamped around me, milking me for my seed. "Do it."

I leaned over her and pressed my lips to her neck, sucking hard as I came inside her.

McKenzie moaned and gripped my shoulders, her fingernails cutting little half-moons into my skin.

It was only fitting she mark me as well.

EIGHT
ALL MINE

McKenzie

When I woke up, I was sprawled over Will. We were naked in the bed on the jet.

And he was inside me.

He was also snoozing quite happily with one arm thrown over his eyes and the other wrapped around my waist. I wondered if we'd passed out while I was riding him.

We'd certainly made love enough times for that to be the case!

I leaned down and kissed his neck, then noticed tiny flecks of blood on the sheets near his shoulder.

"What the...?" I murmured, leaning further to try to get a closer look.

"You're a bit of a wildcat in the sack. You know that, right?" Will rumbled, and I jumped, his cock almost slipping out of me. He put his hands on my hips to prevent that.

"What do you mean?" I asked, making an inadvertent happy sound in my throat when I felt him swelling inside me again.

He chuckled. "You got my shoulders pretty good with those nails of yours."

Nails? I looked down at the sheets again then felt my cheeks heat up. "Oh. Sorry."

"Not a problem. I got you pretty good, too." He sat up so I was straddling his lap and licked a spot on my neck. It stung.

Then I remembered basically begging him to mark me and my whole body turned pink. "Right."

"No need to be embarrassed. It was a real turn-on," he smiled. His hands slid from my hips to cradle my ass.

Will started to help me ride him, and I forgot all about his marks or my marks as I rocked against him, my arms wrapped around his neck.

The pleasure built inside me quickly, my body overstimulated from our previous sex, and I gave a little whimper as I got close to climax.

"It's okay, honeybee. I'm there, too," he groaned.

We came at the same time then kissed and stroked each other as we came down. He didn't pull out right away, which is something I always liked about him.

I was flopped over his chest again, wondering if he was going to want another round and thinking I might be up for it, when there was a knock at the door.

Will grabbed the blanket and yanked it up over us. "What?" he grumbled.

"Door's locked, Will," Ike said cheerfully on the other side.

The man made my skin crawl. "Go away!" I blurted.

A loud, almost sinister laugh followed. "Feisty. I just wanted to let you know you slept through our layover at JFK, and we're due to land in Minneapolis in about an hour. I thought maybe you'd like to… freshen up."

"It's creepy he knows we were sleeping," I whispered to Will.

Will frowned and peered around the bedroom. His eyes fell on the alarm clock next to the bed. "Yes…" he grunted. "Creepy." He yanked the cord out of the wall.

"Aw, what's a surveillance camera or seven between friends?" Ike called through the door.

"Seven?!" I shouted, dragging the blanket closer to my chest. One was awful, but seven?! *Really?!*

"Ike, one of these days, I'm going to gouge your eyes out for looking at what's mine," Will said calmly, stroking a hand up and down my back.

The asshole's chortling increased. I looked up at Will. He was dead serious.

Ike should not have been laughing.

"I'll catch you two in an hour. Do everything I would do." Ike padded away.

I felt gross.

"I'm sorry," Will sighed. He kissed my forehead. "Do you want to take turns in the shower?"

Take turns?! With *that* asshole watching?! "No way in hell!" I protested. "I'm not going anywhere naked without you!"

"I thought you were going to tell me to find all the cameras before you'd get out of bed," he replied, raising an eyebrow in surprise.

"Well, it's not like we can find them all. Or that they're removable. Or that he won't just install more everywhere. I'll bet your house is crawling with them," I said, rather proud of myself for being so calm about it.

He snorted. "You're not wrong. Especially now that I've rebelled. But that doesn't mean it feels great."

"I feel like I want to scratch my skin off. But I'm gonna hold back on that and just make sure I'm never naked without you around. I don't know what that freak will do, and I don't want to find out,' I responded.

Will nodded and very gently pulled out of me. He kissed me as he did so, and I could tell he'd also been hoping for another round. But Icky Ike kind of killed the mood for both of us.

I flipped the covers off us myself. I wasn't going to let that motherfucker beat me down with his seven little cameras!

"There are eight," Will said as I crawled off him and out of bed.

"Eight? What, cameras?!" I gaped.

"At least. He just wanted to enjoy watching us scramble around to find seven, knowing there was at least one more that we'd never find or think to look for," he continued. "It doesn't really matter, but I thought I'd let you know."

I scowled. "Fucker." Then I squared my shoulders and walked butt naked to the bathroom like I was marching in a parade. "You're right. It doesn't matter."

Will chuckled. "That's my girl," he said and followed me in.

TWO ROUNDS of shower sex later, and we were picking clothes up off the floor. Not our old tracksuits, but the clothes Ike had left out for us. They'd become a casualty of sex.

I was trying to find the least wrinkled dress of the four of them while Will did the same with his suits. "I hope these don't come with heels."

"They come with heels," he replied. "I guarantee it. Why, you're not a fan?"

I pulled on a magenta sleeveless dress with a pencil skirt that ended at the knees. "Farm girl. I don't get a lot of opportunities to wear them. They make me wobbly."

"You're going to get plenty of opportunities now. Though I can try to negotiate for flats once we get home." He poked his head in the closet and then swung the door wide, sighing. "All at least three inches. And mostly stilettos."

"You've got to be kidding me." I muscled into the small space that he was occupying and looked down at the side-by-side shoe racks. There were a half-dozen loafers for Will but for me? Eight pairs of heels. "I can't walk in those!"

He stared at the shoes for a while then kissed my cheek. "I won't let you fall."

I was touched. "Thanks."

"Just pick out any pair you want. We just have to get from the jet to the car, then you can take them off again and throw them out the window, if you want." He rubbed the back of his neck. "I'm sorry about this."

I laid my hand over his heart. "Hey, none of it is your fault. You tried to do the right thing, and it backfired. I mean, spectacularly, granted, but it wasn't your fault. I can deal with some cameras and put on some shoes I don't like. I'll live." I kissed him. "I love you."

Will smiled and captured my hand. "I love you, too."

"Now, let's get your tie on. Then we can be ready as soon as we land. The sooner we get off this jet, the sooner we can get to your house and pretend we have privacy," I said.

"Pretend. You're right about that," he muttered.

By silent agreement, I tied his tie, and he helped me into my shoes. I took a step and wobbled right away, my ankle trying to make a break for it.

I frowned. "This is bad."

He straightened his jacket then wrapped an arm around my waist, holding me up. "Better?"

I took a few cautious steps, clamped to his side as he walked with me. "Yeah," I said. "Much."

"Good." He unlocked and opened the pocket door then shifted so he was behind me, holding me by the waist, pressed against his front.

"There you are!" Ike said, looking refreshed and in a different suit than he'd been wearing before. He raised a tumbler full of gold liquid at us. "You both look amazing. Well, good enough, anyway. We might need a stylist to come do your hair and make-up before the next press opportunity, McKenzie, but really, with what you had to work with in that bathroom, you look quite good."

Will got me into a seat by the window, glaring at Ike. "She does look amazing, no stylist needed. And you shouldn't be looking at my woman anyway."

My woman?! My inner feminist burned her bra in protest, but I secretly kind of liked it.

"'My woman'? Well, well, Will, that's something I've never heard come out of your mouth before," Ike chuckled, swirling his drink. "You act like you're so progressive all the time."

"You may progressively kiss my ass, Ike," Will growled. He plopped down next to me on the aisle.

Even though Will had deliberately placed himself between Ike and me, Ike didn't get the hint or didn't care. He wandered over with his drink and sat down directly across from me, a small table the only thing separating us. "Will has been *such* a pain, McKenzie. I'm hoping, with you here, he'll be a much better company executive. He's going to be CEO one day, you know."

"I'm sure he's looking forward to it," I replied, feeling the brush of Ike's shoe against my ankle. I pulled my legs back as far as they would go.

Ike laughed. "I'm sure he isn't, but that's his grandfather's wishes."

"And what do *you* want, Mr. Freeborn?" I asked, wrinkling my nose in disgust as his socked foot traveled up my calf. He must have taken a shoe off. *Ugh.*

"Are you afraid I'm going to try to assassinate Will and take his place?" Ike winked at me while Will tensed beside me.

I took a deep breath and slapped Ike's foot. He'd gotten to my thigh by then. "I'm a little afraid of that, yeah."

"Yes. The proper way to say it is 'yes.' And, sadly, Mr. Masterson had the same idea and has made it impossible for me to inherit the company. But as long as Junior here is around, I get a very, very nice salary," Ike smirked. "And the benefits aren't bad, either."

"Junior was my father," Will said testily. Then he shoved his hand across my lap, grabbed Ike's big toe, and twisted.

There was an unpleasant snap.

Ike yelped. "What the hell?!"

"She's not one of your benefits. And I don't think Grandfather would give a damn if *you* disappeared," Will seethed.

"You are such a fucking bastard, Will!" Ike yowled.

Two bodyguards quickly came over, but, after several deep breaths and a swig of his drink, Ike waved them off.

"I don't think you realize how much of a living hell I can turn your life into," Ike hissed, leaning over the table to get right in Will's face.

"I don't think—" Will began angrily.

I squeezed his hand. "Let's just... cool off, okay guys? Mr. Freeborn has learned his lesson. We don't need to say things to each other that we're both going to regret."

Will and Ike glared at each other, and for a long, tense moment I thought for sure we were screwed, and Ike was going to throw us out the emergency exit.

Then Will sat back, and so did Ike.

"I can't tell whether she's a good influence or a bad influence," Ike murmured, looking at me. "Either way, you didn't give a shit about anything until she came along."

"You're wrong," Will responded, rubbing his thumb along my wrist. I was pretty sure it was to calm himself.

"Oh?" Ike said. "And what else have you *ever* given a shit about besides football?"

"I give a shit that you and Grandfather are running illegal activities that are hurting people," Will growled.

Ike rolled his eyes. "Your ethics are a bigger pain in the ass than you are. Look, it is what it is. You're going to have to suck it up. Or your grandfather will step in, and none of us want that, do we?"

Will squeezed my hand harder and his nostrils flared.

I made a little yip without meaning to.

Will looked at me, then contritely let my hand go. "Sorry," he said softly, patting my knee.

"You're forgiven," Ike smirked.

"I wasn't talking to—" Will snapped.

"Sir?" A flight attendant walked over and addressed Ike. "We're landing in ten minutes."

"Thank you, Ariadne." Ike stood with a wince and hobbled across the aisle to take a different seat. "Our Will here needs a little time to cool down and consider his future... and yours... don't you think, McKenzie? Say, ten minutes?"

I put my hand on Will's thigh to stop him from smarting off. "Sounds like a plan."

Hopefully, ten minutes would be enough.

NINE
NOT ENOUGH

Will

I was fuming.

I held McKenzie's hand for ten minutes while the jet circled, descended, and touched down. The entire time, I could feel her eyes on the side of my face, begging me to be reasonable.

Fuck reason.

That asshole had put his filthy foot on *my woman*, and he expected me to be reasonable?! Fuck that!

"Will..." she whispered to me as the jet taxied to the hangar. "Don't we have to be nice? Aren't you supposed to... you know... make your grandfather happy?"

"The only person in this whole goddamn situation worth making happy is you," I replied hotly, still with a full head of steam.

She leaned her head against my arm. "Don't get me wrong, I think this side of you is kinda sexy. But I'd also really, really like it if we didn't die. That would make me happy."

Anger slowly leached out of me. I squeezed her hand. "Fair point."

The jet stopped, and Ike stood, limping back over to us. "Well, aren't you two cuter than a puddle of puppies?"

The phrase put a bad taste in my mouth. I was convinced this asshole was needling me on purpose. "Don't poke the bear, Ike," I grunted.

He laughed. "But it's so much fun! Especially when there's not a damn thing you can do about it."

"You have nine more toes," I reminded him.

His smile faded into a grimace. "You really were a lot more fun when you were the useless face of the company. At least then I could annoy the fuck out of you by taking over your office, but you didn't give enough of a shit to argue with me."

"That won't be happening anymore." I stood, forcing him further down the aisle so I could help McKenzie out of our row. "I don't give a flying fuck if we have to demolish half the building to make you an office you feel is worthy of your miserable position, but I'm not letting you make a fool out of me to a bunch of mercenaries and arms dealers anymore. You're the one who should be ashamed. Not me."

McKenzie dug her fingers into my arm, warning me to back off.

Ike scowled at me. "And just how do you think you're going to stop me?"

"Simple. I'll just tell Grandfather." I gave him a cold smile. "I just wasn't petty enough to do it before."

"But you are now?" he asked.

"You bet your fucking ass," I replied.

He sighed. "You really are the worst pain in the ass." He glanced at McKenzie.

I didn't like the way he was looking at her. I shifted her behind me. "What?"

"Oh, I was just thinking of telling your grandfather how difficult you've become," he mused, "and wondering just what he'd decide to do about it." His eyes slid to her again.

White hot lightning struck me. One second I was standing with McKenzie at my back, the next I had a hand around Ike's throat.

Bodyguards mobilized immediately from both ends of the plane.

But it was McKenzie grabbing my arm that stopped me from using every hour I'd ever spent at the gym to crush Ike's throat. "Will, no!"

"Mr. Masterson, please let go of Mr. Freeborn," one of the bodyguards said firmly.

"Will." McKenzie gave me a pleading look. "This isn't you."

She was right. It wasn't. But everything in me wanted to be a new and improved Will 2.0. Someone who strangled the life out of the man who threatened the woman I loved. And, honestly, I could have done it. I could have crossed that line.

But then McKenzie would never look at me the same way again.

I released Ike, who coughed and backed away.

Two bodyguards ushered him off the jet. The other four crowded the aisle between us and the exit door, staring me down.

"Are you finished?" the first bodyguard asked me.

I straightened my jacket. "I'm finished."

"Good. There's a limo waiting outside, and the press is just outside the gate. They can see you with a good lens, so I'd suggest keeping it together. Smile. Wave. Get in the limo," he instructed.

"Understood," I replied.

"Let's go." The bodyguard turned and waved the others ahead of him.

It did not escape my notice that two of them peeled off and flanked us from behind. If Ike wanted us to know we were trapped, he was doing a damn good job.

I hoped he'd be unable to speak for a week.

McKenzie stumbled behind me, derailing my vengeful thoughts, and I turned to grab her. She clung to my jacket, looking shaken, but I knew it had nothing to do with the shoes.

"I'm sorry," I whispered, pressing my forehead to hers.

She nodded then managed a brave smile. "It's these heels," she explained to me and the hulking bodyguards around us. "I know you want to support me, Will, but the aisle is so narrow, and I'll bet the stairs are, too."

That's all we needed was for her to twist her ankle and fall down the stairs, doing God only knew what damage to herself. The very idea made my chest seize.

"I'm sorry, Miss Killeen, there isn't a lot we can do..." the first bodyguard began.

"It's Kent—Will!" she squealed as I scooped her up in my arms.

"You're a strong, independent woman, and I respect the hell out of you, but I'm not about to let you break your neck over a pair of shoes. And when we get home, I'm having my stylist get you some flats. Lots of them," I said.

She blushed, and I could see the conflicting viewpoints clashing in her expression. Finally, she slid her arms around my neck and tucked into me so we could get through the door. "I am not comfortable being William Masterson the Third's meek little woman in the press."

"I don't think anyone would ever call you meek," I chuckled. "But just in case anybody was going to get the wrong idea...."

As we stood at the top of the stairs leading down to the tarmac, I fused my lips to hers, kissing her hard.

McKenzie froze, then melted, kissing me back passionately.

Let the press try and say she was 'meek' now!

Then any thought of the press fled my mind as the kiss drew out. Even though we weren't alone, there was a lot of emotion behind that kiss on both sides, and all I knew was that we needed to get somewhere private. Fast.

To talk or screw each other's brains out, I wasn't sure. *Probably both.*

The bodyguard closest to us cleared his throat.

I reluctantly dragged my lips from McKenzie's. "Let's go home," I said, my voice gravelly.

Her chest rose and fell rapidly against mine. Her eyes were filled with heat.

Screw each other's brains out it is.

"You—" She stopped and swallowed, getting the frogginess out of her voice. "You have to get down the stairs first."

I burst out laughing, and a lot of the tension between us and around us dissipated. "True. Well, if something happens, at least we'll break a leg together."

McKenzie held me tightly, and I carried her easily down the stairs. She waved to the press who were behind a distant fence, snapping pictures.

Once the limo door opened, I saw Ike and my smile faded to a frown.

"You were hamming it up just fine for the press. Don't stop now," he rasped, rubbing his throat.

I pasted on a smile, but this one was more fake than Ike's veneers. I set McKenzie down and got her situated in the limo as far from him as possible then got in myself. My smile melted right off. "So, I suppose you'll spin it that I got swept up in a whirlwind romance and went off grid for a while for a honeymoon of sorts?"

"I'd been thinking something along those lines, yes," he replied. He folded his arms across his chest. "I'm very unhappy with you, Will."

"Really? That's a shame. I'm just thrilled with you," I bit back.

McKenzie put a hand on my knee, and I settled, taking her hand and kissing it, all the while glaring mutinously at Ike.

"I really should bring this up to your grandfather," he sighed.

I stiffened.

"But," he said quickly. "I won't. I'll let this one slide. You're still adjusting to the new order of things, and I'd rather not lose an arm for my trouble."

"Thank you," McKenzie interjected. "That's very kind of you."

I ground my teeth.

"Will?" she prompted, nudging my leg with hers. "Aren't we grateful to Mr. Freeborn?"

I growled, not feeling a shred of gratitude.

She nudged me again, giving me a significant look.

"Fine." I didn't want to end up in any kind of position where I wasn't there to protect McKenzie, whether she got taken away or I did. I squared my shoulders and forced my best figurehead-of-the-company smiles. "Thank you, Ike. You're a real pal."

"Thank *you*, Will, for being such a good sport," he replied without missing a beat, smirking.

Someday, I was going to kill this man. Today just wasn't that day.

"Great! Now we're all friends," McKenzie said, giving us both a desperately positive smile.

"Friends," Ike agreed, still smirking. "Now, Will, we need to discuss what happens next."

"Engagement. Marriage. Babies. I'm sure we know the drill," I grunted, still trying to stomach this new 'friends' thing.

Ike snickered. "Of course, there's that. Mr. Masterson Sr. is very pleased to know you're settling down. McKenzie is not an ideal choice, of course, but that can't be helped. We'd have preferred someone of breeding with better social connections..."

"You wanted us to be friends," I reminded him in a clipped tone.

"Just stating the facts. I, for one, like her spirit. I think every family line could use a shot of piss and vinegar," he said, holding up his hands.

"So, besides that, what did you want to discuss with me?" I asked, not really liking the fact that this asshole was rating my woman like a horse in the Kentucky Derby. And not rating her well.

"Business, of course. You've been an excellent face of the company so far, don't get me wrong. Well, except for your little adventure these last months, but we're going to forget about that," he responded. "Your grandfather would like to see you taking on more responsibility."

"I'm not sitting with racists and cutthroats to discuss the price of sex slaves," I growled.

Ike shrugged. "No, not yet. Your grandfather doesn't want you screwing that up. No, you'll be taking over our legitimate contracts. I see it as a win-win, really. You get more experience, and I get about thirty percent of the business taken off my plate so I can concentrate on expanding our... other operations. The more delicate and lucrative ones. Not that I still won't be available to you to give advice or steer you in the right direction."

"Gee, I feel better already," I deadpanned.

"I knew you would," he chuckled. "And then, of course, there are still all your other duties. Charity functions. Gallery openings. The occasional corporate dinner. Press events—"

"I remember my duties, thanks," I said.

He looked at McKenzie. "You don't intend to carry her *everywhere*, do you?"

I put my arm around her. "We're getting her flats."

Ike snorted. "The hell you are. She already looks like a hayseed who's too young for you. The gold digger comments alone are going to be a nightmare. She has to look the part. It's about appearances, Will, you know that."

"I don't give a damn about—" I began.

"I'll get used to them. I have to be, like, some kind of arm candy, right?" she interrupted.

"McKenzie, you don't have to..." I tried.

"Of course she has to. She's going to be Mrs. Masterson, wife of William Masterson the Third. She wears heels. She hosts luncheons. She sits on charitable boards," he said.

"She finishes school," I added firmly. "I'm not budging on that point."

"Oh, she must. At a school and in a program of our choosing." Ike nodded. "Some prestigious, yet useless, degree. But don't worry, McKenzie. You won't be called to use it anyway."

McKenzie swallowed. "Great."

"That's the spirit. Now, let's get you home. You need to start working on the Masterson heir," Ike laughed.

I'd never wanted to punch the smile off someone's face so much in my entire life.

TEN

FROM NOW ON

McKenzie

As Ike spoke, my stomach sank lower and lower. Still, I kept a hold of Will's hand, thinking it might keep him from punching the smug bastard.

"She's nineteen. We're not 'working on the Masterson heir' for another few years yet," Will said, defending me. "And another thing, about college—"

"It's so nice that your grandfather's taking an interest!" I tried defusing that bomb quickly. "I mean, I'd never know what to study to be a proper tycoon's wife."

Will blinked at me.

"See? You can make this very easy, Will. Just like McKenzie here. It can be so painless you'll hardly even feel the sting." Ike purred.

"So, lie back and think of England?" Will replied bitterly.

He wasn't wrong. We were both getting well and truly screwed.

"Something like that, yes," Ike laughed. "And we'll see what your grandfather says about your timeline. Perhaps he'll allow you a few years, at least until our young McKenzie here has finished college. A bachelor's degree."

I could hear Will's teeth scrape against each other. "That sounds great," I said with false brightness. "Wouldn't that be very generous, Will? Letting me finish my studies?"

"Yes, Will, wouldn't that be very generous?" Ike grinned.

"We'll discuss this when we get home," Will said tightly to me.

My eyes widened. Why was he angry at *me* all of a sudden?

"Ooh, the couple's first quarrel. I'm sorry I'll be missing it. We're terribly busy at the office, and I've been away for about two weeks chasing you down. Someone's got to put out the fires. But don't worry, I can catch the highlight reel later." Ike settled back in his seat, folding his hands over his chest as though he'd just had the best dessert after a fine dinner.

"Don't flatter yourself. It's not the first time we've quarreled," Will grumped.

"It's going to be a doozy, though. I can already tell." Ike sighed happily. "You two are going to be hours of entertainment for me. I'll get to watch... everything."

My skin crawled at the idea of Ike watching us have sex. I must have made a face because Ike's eyes lit up, and he added, "There are cameras *everywhere* in that house."

"Thank you, Ike. You're a great buddy," Will grumbled. "I'm —"

"And here we are!" Ike said, cutting Will off mid-sentence.

I looked up just soon enough to watch us pass through a large, wrought iron gate flanked by stone walls. A long driveway led up to what could only be described as a mansion, not a 'house.' I don't know what I'd been expecting, but this wasn't it.

"Pfft," I scoffed despite myself.

"What?" Will and Ike asked together.

"This isn't a house. Oh my God, how out of touch do you have to be...." It was comical. Hysterical.

It was also overwhelming, and the calm I'd been carefully cultivating shattered. I began laughing so hard I had to hold my sides. And I couldn't stop!

"Shit." Will pulled me into his lap and wrapped his arms around me, hugging me tightly. "It's okay, honeybee. Breathe."

"So, if I break it, do I get to buy it?" Ike teased. Or half-teased. He sounded disturbingly serious, actually.

"I swear to Jesus, Ike, if you don't shut your trap, I am going to hit you so hard they're going to have to wire it shut for you!" Will barked. He rocked me gently and rubbed my back. "Let's go inside, okay? We'll get you lying down. I know it's all been a lot. I'm not mad at you. And I hope you're not mad at me. We'll just sit and talk things out—without our friend."

To my horror, I started to cry. Right in front of Ike! I buried my face in Will's jacket and tried to hide it.

"We're going. You go do whatever fucking sicko thing you're going to do," Will said to Ike. To me, he added, "Hang on tight, honeybee."

I kept my face hidden, not wanting Ike to have the satisfaction of thinking he'd broken me. I heard the door open, and my world tilted a little. I heard Will's feet crunch over fine gravel as he carried me, then I bumped against him as he went up a few stairs.

A door opened with a low whoosh.

"Polly," Will said, the name rumbling in his chest. "I'm taking Miss Kent to our room. She is my fiancée. Please treat her exactly as you would if she were my wife."

"Yes, Mr. Masterson," Polly replied. "Shall I get Miss Kent some calming tea?"

"That would be lovely, Polly," he confirmed.

I peeked over Will's shoulder, not sure I wanted Polly seeing me cry, either, but curious about her nonetheless. She was a woman in her late forties with blonde hair that was just starting to go silver. She was short and stout and seemed pleasant enough.

"Don't trust her. All the staff is hand-picked by Grandfather," Will murmured in my ear.

That doused any hope I had of making a friend. "Oh."

"And we are going to talk after you've had a rest and some tea," he stated.

"Oh," I repeated. "How... very British."

He laughed a little. Another door swung open, and then he deposited me gently on a large bed. The duvet felt like a cloud!

"Okay, honeybee. You just relax. Let's get these ridiculous shoes off you." He reached down and slid my heels off, dumping them on the floor.

My dress suddenly felt too tight—well, not suddenly. It'd felt tight since I'd put it on, which I think it was supposed to. But now, I just couldn't catch my breath. I struggled to get my arms behind me to unzip it.

Will slid his arms around me and pulled the zipper down, brushing my back with his knuckles. "Better?" he asked softly.

"Better." I wriggled a bit to loosen the fabric, then took a few deep breaths. "Um... sorry I freaked out."

"I'm surprised you didn't sooner. Sorry I was an overbearing, violent, Neanderthal asshole," he responded, sitting down next to me and twining his fingers with mine.

I gave a very undignified snort that would probably have made the social media rounds if we'd been in public. "You're just mad I didn't let you snap Ike's turkey neck."

He laughed. "It is kind of a turkey neck, isn't it? Yes, I'm a little upset about that. But you did the right thing, and I did the wrong thing. I could have caused you a lot of pain, and I'm sorry."

"So, this is us not talking until I've rested and had some tea?" I joked.

Will stroked my face, and I felt a lot of my panic subside. "This is just the prequel. We've got a lot of ground to cover later." He leaned down and kissed me. "But that can wait."

"Okay." *God, this mattress is nice.* I let my eyes close for a moment.

Just a moment.

"MISS KENT?" a familiar voice asked.

I blinked my eyes open to see Polly leaning over me. "Holy shit!"

She took a step back. "I'm sorry to disturb you, Miss Kent, but Mr. Masterson had to take a call. His grandfather."

Confused, I asked, "What does that have to do with you waking me up?"

"I just thought now would be a good time for us to talk." She sat down on the bed beside me. "Without others listening. Well, the wrong others."

"Without Will listening," I said, sitting up and scooting to the edge of the bed so we were sitting next to each other.

"Precisely." She patted my knee. "I'm just worried that, since you've never been in a situation like this before, you might be confused about the rules."

"Rules?" I echoed.

Polly nodded. "I can tell Mr. Masterson is very devoted to you. Certainly more than any of his other women, and to call you his fiancée! Oh my."

I had the feeling she wanted me to ask about the 'other women.' But I didn't. Will had been very clear on that point, and besides, if I wanted to know about the 'other women' that badly, I'd make him tell me. I didn't want to hear a damn thing from her. "I guess that's what you call the person you're going to marry," I replied instead.

Her expression soured. "Young lady, you're nothing but a gold digger. Pure and simple. You're immature, which is understandable given your age. But you are also unrefined and a little bit stupid, if you don't mind my saying."

"No, please, don't hold back on my account," I said sweetly.

She shrugged. "I won't. You don't belong here. You certainly don't belong with Mr. Masterson."

"I know." I watched as the words threw her off balance.

"You... know?" she repeated.

With a grin as wide as the Montana sky, I said, "It's an arranged marriage."

Polly's jaw went slack. "Arranged?"

"Yes. By Mr. Masterson Sr. You didn't know?" I asked, feigning shock.

"No, I—"

"Rest assured, I'll make sure to share your opinions on my suitability with him. I'm sure he wouldn't want his grandson marrying someone immature, unrefined, and stupid," I said.

That was the moment she realized how badly she'd screwed up. "Please don't."

"Why not? You were happy enough to tell me what you thought. If your opinion matters so much, surely Mr. Masterson Sr. wants to hear it," I responded pleasantly.

Her face went pasty white.

I dropped my cheerful façade and leaned close to her. "Will's on the phone with his grandfather right now, isn't he? Why waste time? I'll go find him, and we can get this over with."

When I went to stand, she gripped my knee. "Miss Kent—"

"Maybe you'd know me better as Miss Killeen." I brushed her hand aside.

What I suspected turned out to be true. She gasped. "He would never allow such a thing."

"Why not? It's strategic. Puts me publicly with Will so I can't disappear like my parents did. Gets my parents off his back because they won't do anything to Mr. Masterson Sr. if they think it will blow back on me. It's, well, a *master*ful stroke, really." I smiled at my little pun, even while knowing everything coming out of my mouth was true. It did not inspire good feelings about the situation.

And, I realized I hadn't really thought about my parents in a while. I'd been too preoccupied with my own problems.

"It... does make sense," she wheezed, bringing me out of my dark cloud.

"I know, right? What's inconvenient about this whole thing is that Will and I actually do love each other very much. And we're going to be as goddamn happy as we can be. I will do *anything* to make sure of that. So, why don't you get your interfering, insulting, uppity ass to the kitchen and bring me my tea?" I suggested angrily.

Polly scrambled to her feet. "You won't say anything to Mr. Masterson Sr.?"

"No. But I will to Mr. Masterson the Third." I held up a hand when she began to protest. "I'm going to tell him not to involve his grandfather, but I need him to know he's being disrespected in his own home, and that I am, too. He already told me not to trust you. Thanks for adding the final nail to that coffin."

"I'm sorry. I'm very sorry. I'll get you your tea," she said glumly and trudged off.

I sat back down on the bed and scrubbed my face with my hands, wanting to scream.

Is there no one in this world we can trust?!

Will

"Grandfather," I said tersely into my newly-acquired phone as I paced the arboretum, "I told you I'd do whatever you ask. I'm back. You've got me on a tight leash. I get it. If I don't do what you want, McKenzie's going to suffer. You don't need to call and confirm it with me. Shouldn't you be saving your phone calls for your lawyer?"

William Masterson Sr. just laughed. It chilled me even more than it had when he told me I wouldn't be a football star. "I thought you could use the reminder. I might be... away for a while. But that doesn't mean I don't have eyes on you." His voice hardened. "You are allowed your one rebellion. And I'll even give you your McKenzie. But I swear, William, if you pull something like this again...."

"I know." He wouldn't be stupid enough to say it on a prison phone. A threat, even from someone as prestigious as William Masterson Sr., would have to be taken seriously and could hurt his appeal.

An appeal that would almost certainly go through now that the two key witnesses were in the wind.

Damn it!

"I'm glad you know. Now, I expect you to bring your young lady to see me this weekend. It's been too long since we've sat and had a nice conversation. I hear she's very... spirited." He chuckled.

"I don't think she'll be agreeable to that," I replied, anger roiling in my gut. The old man wanted to rub it in our faces that he owned us. In person.

"Make her agreeable," my grandfather said firmly. "I want to see the girl who's going to be the mother of my great-grandchildren."

I dragged in a breath and let it out slowly. "Is that really necessary?"

"Yes. Now, do as I say like the good grandson I know you are," he said.

It was an order.

"I'll let her know we have weekend plans," I responded, gripping the phone hard.

"Good. I'll see you this weekend. Until then, Ike's in charge. He'll steer you both in the right direction," he said sweetly and hung up.

I was about to chuck the phone when McKenzie came around the rhododendrons. I pocketed the phone instead, my rage dissipating. "Honeybee, did you sleep well?" I asked, opening my arms to her.

She walked right in and hugged my waist, laying her cheek against my chest. "I did. Sorry, I didn't mean to fall asleep on you. I know you wanted to talk."

"You needed sleep more." I tilted her chin up and kissed her.

McKenzie kissed me back, and I nearly forgot everything I'd wanted to talk to her about. But, my grandfather's veiled threats festered in the back of my mind, and I finally broke away, setting her at arm's length.

"Will?" She looked hurt and confused.

"Much as I'd like to ravish you right here and now, I do need to talk to you. Well, with you. Actually, both," I said. "And if I have you in my arms, every other thought is going to go out the window."

"Oh." She gave a little laugh. "That's understandable, I guess."

I smiled at her. "I thought you'd understand." I looked around, then brought her over to a sitting area and settled us on a white, wrought iron bench. "All right, so... where to begin...."

"You don't want me getting between you and Ike?" she suggested.

I frowned. "Yes, there is that."

"Never gonna happen. I'm not losing you because you go to prison for killing him," she said, holding a hand over my mouth when I would have argued. "End of discussion."

Gently, I took her hand away from my mouth. "You won't be there when we're at work together."

"Then you'll just have to behave yourself, won't you?" She sniffed. "But you know he's doing it on purpose, right? He's trying to get a rise out of you using me, and it's working. Stop giving him what he wants!" She swatted me.

I captured her hand, feeling a little foolish, but mostly just pissed off at Ike. "I'm hoping he's realized what he wants is to die if he keeps it up. It's bad enough we're all tied up with nowhere to go and no one to help us. I'm not letting him take advantage of that—of you. You shouldn't have to put up with his... lasciviousness."

"You paused before the big word. Afraid the hayseed wouldn't understand it?" she asked.

That was a complete one-eighty. "Honeybee, what are you talking about?"

McKenzie sighed. "Sorry. Nothing. It doesn't have anything to do with you. I mean it does, but it's not your fault."

"Now you're going to have to explain because I'm confused," I said.

She shifted uncomfortably. "It's just... people keep saying I'm not refined enough for you."

"People? Who, Ike?" I asked, still lost.

"Yeah, Ike. Or is it 'yes'?" she snarked.

I shook my head and held her eyes with mine. "It's whatever the fuck you want it to be. I don't care."

"I mean, I know you don't care," she said. "But other people do."

"When did you start giving a shit about other people's opinions?" I asked. "McKenzie, I don't know who's been saying what to you, but you can tell them to go fuck themselves. You're perfect just the way you are. And you're perfect for me."

She made a face. "That was very cheesy."

"And it was very true. So stop worrying about that bullshit." I kissed her nose. "Though... who besides Ike has been bothering you about crap like that?"

McKenzie shrugged. "I guess I told her I was going to tell you. Polly cornered me in your bedroom—"

"Our bedroom," I corrected her. "But go on." I could already feel the coals of anger she'd helped to quench getting stirred up again.

"She basically said I wasn't fit to be your fiancée. Don't worry about it, though. I already told her off."

My anger turned to humor. "I thought you might have. My honeybee's not a wilting flower, after all."

She laughed. "Can't say that I am, no."

"Do you want me to fire her?" I asked, stroking her arm. "I can, you know. Grandfather would be pissed if he knew that there was a staff member bad-mouthing his future granddaughter-in-law."

McKenzie made a face. "Don't remind me. No, I don't want you to fire her. I've got that to threaten her with, and it's not like we'd have the same leverage with a new staff member. It can't hurt for Polly to owe us a favor."

"True. Though I don't know whether to be proud or appalled that you're getting so good at playing this game," I replied sadly, touching her cheek.

She kissed my palm. "Be proud. I want to be able to help you any way I can. Like a real partner."

"You are a real partner to me." I sighed and pulled her into my lap.

"I thought you were worried about not being able to keep your hands off me long enough to have a conversation." She giggled, looping her arms around my neck.

"I am," I admitted. "But I want you near me for the next part."

McKenzie looked surprised. "Wow, it must be something big if being right next to you wasn't close enough."

"It is." I took a deep breath. "Grandfather wants us to visit him this weekend."

She stared at me. "You're kidding. At the prison?"

I nodded. "It wasn't really a request. More of a directive."

"So... we *have* to go," she said slowly.

"Yes." I buried my face in her shoulder and made a frustrated sound. "I'm sorry. There's nothing I can do about it, and yes, I'm pretty sure he just wants to gloat. I—"

McKenzie gently took my face in her hands. "Then we just go."

"We just go?" I blinked. "Simple as that?"

"It's not like we can avoid him forever. Without my parents, he'll be getting out of prison soon," she said bitterly. "I'd like to face him somewhere he can't get his hands on me."

My eyes narrowed. "He is never getting his hands on you."

"He already kind of has." She made a vague gesture at our surroundings.

I looked around at our gilded cage, feeling trapped and hating it.

She leaned in and whispered in my ear. "We are getting out of here, though."

"We're—" I replied, startled. "We're what now?"

"Shh! We'll need to play his game for now, but we're going to escape. You just wait. We'll come up with a plan—" she continued excitedly.

I grabbed her by the arms. "McKenzie, you can't talk about things like that here," I hissed, glancing around. Was that a camera behind the cherub sculpture? In the rose bushes? Under the bench?

Suddenly, everything looked as though it was watching us.

"But we will," she insisted, still keeping her voice low.

"Not now. Not here," I replied. My voice was tense even in my ears.

She made an exasperated noise. "Shower?" she suggested.

It was as good a place as any, but I was fairly certain we'd be surveilled there as well. I slid her off my lap and took her hand, dragging her along as I took quick strides to get us back to my bedroom.

"Will, slow down!" she protested, jogging to keep up.

I didn't want to slow down. I wanted us to be safe, and nowhere was safe. Nowhere.

When I swung open the heavy wooden door to my bedroom, Polly was tidying up inside. Ostensibly. I gave her a stern look and she jumped.

"Mr. Masterson!" Polly cast around for an excuse, and I knew for certain she was not there to clean. "I was just—"

"Leave," I said coldly.

She nodded vigorously. "Yes, of course, Mr. Masterson. If you need me—"

"I won't." I slammed the door after she scampered out.

"Will..." McKenzie said.

I took her hand again and yanked her into the bathroom and right into my large, multi-jet shower. I turned on every one, including the big rain shower head, while we were both fully clothed.

McKenzie gasped and hugged herself as cold water hit her. "Will, what's gotten into you?!"

"Do you want to get yourself killed?!" I yelled with more force than I meant to. "Do you?!"

"I... I was just saying we're going to get out of here. I mean, we are. Eventually. You... believe that, right?" she asked, her eyes wide and hurt.

I raked a hand through my hair, my suit jacket becoming heavy as it got soaked. I hadn't even remembered I was wearing one. "I don't know."

"You don't know?!" She looked as though I'd hit her.

"I don't. I don't know for sure, okay?" I shrugged out of my jacket, letting it fall to the shower floor with a wet plop.

"Damn, Will, lie to me! Give me some hope," she snapped, beginning to shiver. Her dress was now plastered to her, hugging every curve.

"Fuck. Fuck this fucking water," I muttered, turning to play with the temperature dials. And to keep my brain on track. Nearly-naked McKenzie was always going to distract me.

She slapped my hands away from the dials. "Don't turn your back on me after dropping that bomb on me!"

"I'm not turning my back on you!" I frowned.

McKenzie raised an eyebrow at me.

"Not because... never mind. It's not important. I just want us to stop talking about this, okay? Just... not in this house. Fuck, probably not anywhere," I said.

Tears shimmered in her eyes. "You're just going to lie down and let this happen?"

Guilt stabbed me in the chest, but I had to make her stop. "I didn't say that. I'm just saying—"

"Saying what?! What could be more important than getting out of here?!" she shouted in my face.

"Keeping you alive, goddammit!" I shouted back.

TWELVE

KEEP ME SAFE

McKenzie

Even though we were in the shower, I could tell he was sweating. Will's face was flushed even though the water was freezing. His words echoed around the large bathroom, bouncing off the expensive black tile.

"That's not good enough," I replied, moving my hands to my hips. I instantly regretted that decision. The water was still cold, and it hit my chest again, my formerly warm nipples freezing through my dress.

Will's eyes flicked to my chest. I realized my nipples were probably putting on a nice show, but I wasn't backing down now. I raised my chin. "Are you listening to me?"

"I heard you," he replied testily, meeting my eyes again. "And I don't care what you say, keeping you alive is damn well good enough for me."

"And I'm telling you just staying alive isn't good enough!" I argued, stepping closer and poking him in the chest. "That's not living."

He took my hand in both of his. "McKenzie, we've only been

here a day. I'm sure some opportunity might present itself, but talking about it openly in the house is suicide! Do you want Ike to overhear us? My grandfather? What do you think they'll do to you if they think you're being a bad influence?"

I understood his point, but I still didn't like it. I didn't like how they were going to use me to control Will, to make him someone he wasn't. All I could see in our future was Will being ground down more and more every day until he was a mere shell of the man I'd fallen in love with. I couldn't bear the thought.

"So what if they know?" I doubled down. "They don't expect us to just sit around playing checkers while they play with our lives, do they? So we don't discuss actual plans with them or in this house. But we at least make sure they know we're not broken. They haven't broken us, Will. They haven't broken... you." I searched his tired blue eyes. "Have they?"

He let go of my hand. "Why would you even say that?"

"I want to know," I said desperately, hugging myself to him, my arms going around his waist, my cheek pressed against his soaked shirt. A shirt that left nothing to the imagination, but I couldn't be distracted. Not now. "I need to know you're still with me. That we're a team. That we'll get out of this together. Please, Will, don't give up now!"

He sighed and gently pushed me off him, turning away for a moment.

My heart shattered.

He fiddled with the dials some more, then the water became blessedly warm.

I couldn't have cared less.

"McKenzie," he murmured, "what makes you think I've given up?"

"It's written all over your face," I responded, defeated. "And just... the way you're so focused on keeping me alive instead of figuring out how to get out of here. And the way you talk to Ike. I mean, you did break his toe, which was a little reckless and also kind of cool, but that's beside the point. I don't... I don't want to be the reason you give up your integrity. Your life."

There it was. The whole truth of it.

Will sighed. "I would give up a lot more than that to keep you alive."

"See?!" I said, my teary gaze snapping up. "That's exactly what I don't w—"

He put a finger over my lips. "I'm not thinking about me. I'm thinking about you."

I pulled his hand away. "Exactly! That's—"

"And I know you can't thrive here," he interrupted me.

"No, I can't! I—wait, where is this going?" I asked, feeling we'd taken a sharp turn somewhere.

Will stroked my wet hair. "If I can't get me out, I'm at least getting you out. But it's going to take some time. And I don't want Grandfather to know my plan, though he probably knows it already."

"What do you mean, if you can't get you out?" I replied, rage bubbling up in me as realization dawned. I was suddenly pummeling his chest with my fists. "Will Masterson *the Third*, I am *not* leaving here without you!"

"McKenzie, this is important. This is a very grown-up thing, okay? I'm making my choice, and—" he began.

"I reject your choice! And your 'grown-up' logic! Don't you ever speak to me like that!" I shouted back. I was crying now for real, my chest heaving with suppressed sobs. "I'm nineteen years old! I have just as much right to make my own decision as you do!"

He finally caught my wrists, stopping me from using him as a human timpani. "Yes," he acknowledged. "But I am eleven years older than you...."

"Screw that." I struggled in his grip, but though it was gentle, it was also strong. "You think I care how much older you are than me? News flash—I don't. I don't think it matters one bit. And if you think you can just make choices for me, then I'd have to say you were eleven years *younger* than me because you should know better by now."

Will stared at me. Then he started to laugh. "This is ridiculous."

"You're right. It is. Your plan is stupid," I said.

"You haven't even heard it yet!" he protested.

"It doesn't involve both of us getting out of here, therefore, it is stupid." I tugged my wrists, but he didn't let go.

Instead, he used his hold on me to turn me into him, holding me against him with my back to his chest.

"Feel better now?" he asked, nuzzling my neck.

"Oh no. Acting all sweet is not getting you out of this one, mister," I grouched back, bonking my head against his jaw.

He laughed again. "Is my honeybee pissed off?"

"Yeah, and she's gonna sting you if you don't knock it off," I warned.

Will sighed and dropped his chin onto my hair. "I don't want you to get hurt. If you stay with me, you're going to get hurt."

"We're not even going to be here that long anyway," I said. I knew I sounded painfully optimistic, but I didn't want either of us to lose hope.

"We could be," he mumbled. "We could be here a very long time. Even if we did follow my plan, getting you out will take... months. Maybe even years!"

"And, again, I say that is a stupid plan." I turned so I could look at him. "We need a better plan."

He hugged me tighter. "We're not coming up with it here and now."

"No, but we're keeping an open mind," I practically ordered him.

Will smiled, and it was a bit sad. It made my heart break all over again. "All right, honeybee. I'll keep an open mind."

"That's all I ask." I reached up and touched his cheek. I wanted to shake him, but more than that, I wanted to re-establish our bond.

With a groan, he lowered his lips to mine.

I let his kiss ignite me, from the top of my head to the tips of my toes.

"Is it so bad that I want to take care of you?" he whispered in my ear, kissing along the shell and down my neck.

"Don't go all caveman on me now. We're a team, remember?" I replied, shivering when his knuckles grazed my back as he lowered the zipper on my dress.

"Unga-unga, me Will. You honeybee. Me take you back to cave," he teased.

I rolled my eyes. "You're hopeless, you know that?"

"Hopelessly in love with somebody, I know," he quipped. He smoothed my sleeves down my arms. I gave a little shimmy, and my dress fell to the shower floor in a wet heap, leaving me in my bra and underwear.

His eyes sparked fire as he looked at me in my see-through under-garments. He reached out and gently pinched my nipples.

I moaned and leaned my forehead on his shoulder. "W-What are you planning t-to do when we g-get back to this cave?"

Will nibbled my collarbone, still rolling my nipples between his thumb and forefinger. He very kindly slipped his leg between mine so I had something to grind against while he took his sweet time with me. "Show honeybee my big club."

I laughed, lowering my hands to the front of his pants. "Do I get to see your big club?" I unzipped his pants and stuck my hands in.

He groaned. "You bet your ass you do." He put his hand over mine and encouraged me to set him free. Which I did. Gladly.

His big friend was leaking, it was so happy to see me.

"Don't stare at him like that. He'll only get a bigger ego," Will joked.

"We wouldn't want that," I replied and stroked up and down his shaft.

He grunted and backed me to the shower wall, pressing his fist against the tile as I teased him mercilessly.

"Problems?" I asked innocently.

"A few. But only one I can take care of right now." He reached down and ripped my panties open.

I snorted. "Good thing you're rich because you're awfully hard on my wardro—"

Will removed my hand from his cock and lifted me up onto it, sheathing himself deep inside me while pressing me against the wall.

I wrapped my legs around his waist out of instinct then held on for dear life as he began screwing me hard against the tile.

His mouth sought mine, and we shared a passionate kiss while his hips ground against mine, sending delicious zings of pleasure throughout my body.

He must have known when I was close because he broke the kiss. "Say my name," he commanded me.

"W-Will!" I cried, coming hard around him. My inner muscles gripped his cock, begging him to release inside me.

He came with a shout, grinding his hips against mine so he was as deep as he could go when he did so.

I was pretty sure I was going to have some bruises on my back from the tile, but I didn't care. I panted with my head on Will's shoulder, holding him tightly. And he held me just as tightly.

"Did you get your caveman out?" I asked after a while.

"Well, I did get to show you my club. I suppose I should be satisfied with that for now," he said, running his fingers through my wet hair.

"You want to finish showering and move this to the bedroom, don't you?" I responded with a grin.

Will laughed. "You know me so well."

I poked him in the nose. "Stop being a caveman, and we can discuss it."

"Discuss it?" he sounded almost horrified. "Just discuss it?"

"Cavemen who decide to make unilateral decisions—yes, Ike, I know big words—without consulting their partners don't get nookie," I said primly.

He groaned and carefully pulled out of me, setting me on my

feet. "McKenzie, I don't even know if my plan will work. And if I can get it to work, it'd take at *least* a year. I'm also not sorry about wanting to get you out, whether or not I get out, too."

"That's fine, then. I think we can find a way out of this in the next three months," I replied with confidence. I patted his chest. "So your plan won't even matter."

Will smacked his forehead on the tile. "McKenzie...."

"Trust me. Everything is going to be fine. We'll figure a way out of this," I assured him.

THIRTEEN

PARTIES AND POSSIBILITIES

Will

I wished I shared her optimism.

We finished showering, cleaning up after our lovemaking, then went to the bedroom where I thought Mr. Caveman would get to do a little more cave diving. Instead, we both stared at formal attire laid out on the bed, put there while we were in the shower.

"Okay, that's creepy," McKenzie said, and I nodded my agreement.

A heavy vellum envelope was lying on top of my suit. I picked it up and pulled out an invitation to a dinner and auction for a charity I knew. We were one of its top donors, in fact.

I had to laugh. "You've got to be shitting me."

She took the invitation from me. "'Comunidades en Común'?"

"Yes. 'Communities in Common,'" I translated. "It's a charitable organization that helps starving children in Central America pursue their education to try to elevate them and their families out of poverty."

"Why is that funny?" she asked.

"Because those are the very communities we target to abduct

women and children into the illegal slave trade," I answered, grimacing at the invitation in her hand. "I can't believe they expect us to go. The hypocrisy...."

McKenzie looked from the invitation to me and back again. "Should I rip it up?"

"No. We're going to need it to get into the event," I sighed.

"But you just said you don't want to go," she said, confused.

I plucked the invitation from her hand and tucked it in the lapel pocket of the suit jacket lying on the bed. "Ike, and more importantly Grandfather, will take a very dim view if we don't go."

"We can't have that, I suppose." She huffed, looking down at her dress. She picked up the green gown with shimmery bits and turned it this way and that. "It's got an open back."

"It does," I observed, looking it over myself. "Is that a problem?"

She wrinkled her nose. "I won't be able to wear a bra."

"Oh." I looked at the fabric again and gave it a little tug. It seemed sturdy and opaque enough. "Try it on. Let's see if it will be a problem."

"Hmm. Okay." She found stockings—with a garter belt—and lace panties on the bed as well and began pulling them on.

My mouth went dry when I saw the garter belt.

"Can you help me with this?" she asked, much to my delight.

I knelt down next to her and helped to get her in her stockings, sliding my fingers along her soft skin as I did so.

McKenzie poked me in the forehead. "No funny business. We don't have time."

"More's the pity," I lamented, then kissed the inside of her thigh before standing and patting her on the ass. "You're all set. Do you want help with the dress as well?"

"Probably zipping it up, but I think I can do the rest." She shimmied into the dress, which fit her perfectly and clung iridescently in all the right places. "I'm not sure whether to be grossed out or impressed that somebody knows my measurements."

"Honestly, I was thinking the same thing," I admitted. I stroked my hand down her open back. "Still, you look very sexy. I'm going to have a hard time concentrating on anything else all night."

She giggled. "Good. Then you won't have to think about how pissed off you are that Ike is sending us to this thing, even though it's completely hypocritical."

I pulled her to me, still completely naked, and kissed her hard. "You could make me forget my own name."

"I guess I'll have to give you a new one, then," she said. She sobered and brushed my hair back with her fingertips. "Are you going to be okay? Really?"

I took her hand and kissed her fingers one by one. "Honestly? It's going to be rough. I suppose I'll get used to it over time. But this is the first time I'll have attended one of these things since finding out what we *really* do."

McKenzie wrapped her arms around me, the diaphanous fabric of her open sleeves brushing against my skin as she did so. "I'll be there. We can get through it together. And Will?"

"Yes?" I replied, holding her tightly.

"I don't ever want you to get used to it," she said fiercely. "I want it to always bother you when we go to these things."

I nodded. "I don't think that will be much of a problem."

"Good." She pulled back slightly. "I suppose I should let you get dressed. Unless it's a masquerade dinner, and we're going as *The Emperor's New Clothes*."

"I'd... really rather not," I replied. I kissed her one last time then began dressing. "There's probably make-up in your exact colors in the bathroom by now."

"Like I said—creepy." She went into the bathroom. I could see her rummaging through the cabinets and the shock on her face when she found what she was looking for. "Oh my God, it even has my name on it!"

"What does?" I asked, searching around the bed until I found the cufflinks I was sure someone had already picked out for me. Maybe Polly. Or Ike himself.

I really hoped it had been Polly.

"This huge make-up case! Well, I mean, it has my initials. Kind of. It has 'MKM,'" she said, opening the case and taking items out to look at them. "I'm not sure what the other 'M' is...?"

"'McKenzie Kent/Killeen Masterson,'" I deduced.

She dropped a lipstick. "Holy shit! You're right!"

I went into the bathroom and scooped the lipstick off the floor, handing it back to her. "It was an easy guess. Ike laid it all out for us on the way here."

"Yeah, I should have guessed that, too." She looked down at her dress. "Damn, am I supposed to put the make-up on *before* the dress?"

"Oh. Yes, I think you are." I felt like a complete moron. I'd been so busy fantasizing about getting her back out of the dress that I'd forgotten the natural order of things.

McKenzie laughed. "I guess you'll have to get me out of it again, then."

I groaned. "Yes, but I was hoping I'd be able to do a lot more when that time came."

"Too bad, so sad." She turned her back to me so I could undo the zipper at her waist. Once she stepped carefully out of the dress, she tossed it to me to hold.

My punishment for my lapse in judgment was to watch her apply her make-up, breasts bouncing, ass wiggling, and standing in those infernal stockings.

"Didn't any of the women who stayed here get ready for the day in front of you?" she asked suddenly.

I frowned, not liking the direction this was taking. "I thought we agreed we weren't going to talk about that. And you make it sound like this was Grand Central Station."

"Sorry." She carefully applied eyeliner.

I didn't say anything for a while because I didn't want her to poke herself in the eye. When she finished her mascara, I said, "Are you really that worried about the other women I've had in my life?"

She blushed. I could see that even under the natural tones she'd applied to her cheeks. "I mean, I try not to think about it. I don't generally think of myself as a jealous woman. But, I don't know. We're here. This is your room."

"Our room," I corrected her.

"Well, yeah, our room. But it was your room, and I imagine there were women here," she continued. "And tonight we're going to this dinner where I'm sure people have seen you with different women on your arm. You know, women who aren't me. There might even be some of them there, right? The 'right kind' of woman who travels in your circles?"

"You're the only 'right kind' of woman I've ever met," I said fiercely. "I don't give a flying fuck what Ike said. And let me tell you about those other women who travel in my circles. Most of them are petty, spoiled, trophy wives in training. Not one of them caught my attention for more than three months. I was shallow. They were pretty and could be bought. I had needs. That was it. And that's the sum total of it."

McKenzie nodded, and I saw her eyes shimmer.

"Oh, honeybee." Careful not to smudge her make-up, I put my arms around her and grabbed some tissues, dabbing gently at her eyes. "Are you nervous about going out with me and running into someone I dated before?"

"A little," she acknowledged. She glanced in the mirror and sighed. "I'm going to have to do the eyeliner all over again."

"Hey. Look at me." I tilted her chin up with one finger. "You have nothing to worry about. I'll be with you the whole time. Your speech is fine. Your age is something they'll judge me for, not you. You're intelligent, beautiful, and kind. Not one of those women can hold a candle to you."

She gave me a watery smile. "I love you."

"I love you, too. And I'd prefer to stay here and watch you bounce up and down on my dick in that garter belt and stockings, while I tell you how many million virtues you possess. But that's going to have to wait." I slid my hand over her bare breast.

McKenzie laughed and swatted it away. "You're incorrigible!"

"You keep saying that like it surprises you," I grinned.

"Mhm. Come on, handsome, we need to get ready." She turned back to the mirror and began reapplying her eyeliner.

"I am ready. Someone decided to get me all hot and bothered," I replied archly.

She scoffed. "Same."

"So," I said, "are you going to tell me about your boyfriends now?" I regretted saying it, mostly because she poked herself in the eye with the pencil. "Sorry, sorry!"

McKenzie winced, dabbed her eye with a Kleenex, then looked over at me. "You have terrible timing, you know that?"

"That's not what you say in bed." I tried brightening the mood.

She wasn't having it. "I suppose it's only fair, though it's not like you gave me a number."

"I'm not giving you a number. I'm eleven years older than you. It wouldn't be fair," I insisted.

"Fine, fine. Well, I can. Just two. Two guys. I mean, three if you count my middle school boyfriend, but that was just puppy love. I never slept with him," she said thoughtfully. "My high school boyfriend was my first. Totally cliché. We thought it would be so special on prom night. It was awful. Awkward, painful, the whole works. The boyfriend I had last year in college was better, but he was always on his phone and forgetting birthdays and Valentine's Day and things like that. I decided I deserve better."

"You do deserve better," I responded. I waited for her to finish with her eyeliner then took her hands. "I feel kind of bad being just the third guy you've been with after those two turds. I have... a lot more experience. I'm past my awkward years—I hope. Don't you want to experience all that?"

"All what?" she asked.

I shrugged. "All the trials and tribulations. Finding out who you really are and what—and who—you really want. All—"

"Will, please shut up before I smack you," she groaned. She squished my cheeks so I was making a fish mouth and couldn't talk anymore. "I know who I am, and I know what I want. I know people change. I know I will change. I know you will, too. Hopefully, we change in a complimentary sort of way."

It made sense. Or rather, it at least kept the little flame of guilt in me under a nice pile of dirt. I didn't care if that dirt turned out to be bullshit. I loved McKenzie. She loved me.

That was all that mattered.

FOURTEEN
WEIGHED AND MEASURED

McKenzie

Ike chose heels again, of course. On the one hand, they were quite pretty and matched the dress perfectly. On the other hand, I was still wobbly.

"I'm going to look like such a fool," I murmured to Will as we exited the limo and headed up the hotel stairs. Slowly. With me clinging to him like a lichen.

He patted my hand, which had a death grip on his arm. "I'm not leaving your side."

"You have to at some point. Bathroom. Pompous rich old fart needing a word," I grumbled, wincing when my ankle almost gave. I was going to fall on these stone steps before we even made it into the building!

"If I have to talk to some 'pompous rich old fart,' I'll make sure you're seated at a table," he said, suppressing a chuckle. I could hear it in his voice.

I swatted him with my clutch, which also matched the dress. "It's not funny!"

"I'm not laughing at your predicament. I'm laughing at the 'pompous rich old fart,'" he assured me.

"Don't tell me you don't know a few." I sounded grumpy. I was. *Damn Ike and these shoes!*

"Will!" A boisterous voice broke through the chatter as we finally made it to the top of the stairs. Sure enough, a balding, red-faced man in his seventies with a woman who could have been his granddaughter dangling off his arm came pushing through the crowd.

"Don't laugh," Will muttered to me, even though I could tell he was trying very hard not to laugh himself. "Don't."

I bit down hard on my lower lip. "I'm not laughing," I mumbled.

"Uh-huh." Will walked us over to the man and his arm candy.

"It's been an age!" the man said, forcefully taking Will's hand and shaking it. "Where have you been?"

I leaned heavily on Will while he smiled down at me. "I've just been with McKenzie here. It was a whirlwind romance. McKenzie, this is Leopold Cross of Cross and Cross Ltd. Leopold, this is McKenzie Kent."

"Soon to be McKenzie Masterson, if the rumor mill is to be believed." Leopold chuckled and ribbed Will with his elbow. "My, and she is a pretty little thing. Maybe Gretchen here will be the next Mrs. Cross. What do you think?"

"Gwendolyn," the young woman corrected sourly. Then she turned on her full charm mode. "You really think so, pookie?" She batted her eyelashes at him.

"It's always a possibility, sugar." Leopold smiled. He leaned into Will and whispered so loudly it was impossible for Gwendolyn and me not to hear. "They really lap it up, don't they? Sad they don't know there will be a new one next week."

She pursed her lips.

It occurred to me then that she wasn't much older than me, if she even was older than me.

"I think McKenzie and I could use some champagne," she announced, reaching out and tugging on my arm.

It forced me to take a step, and my ankle wriggled like a fish was trying to escape my leg. "Eek!"

Gwendolyn noticed and stopped. "Let's go like this," she said softly and wrapped my arm through hers so she was holding me up.

"In point of fact, Leopold, though we haven't made a formal announcement yet, McKenzie and I will be tying the knot," Will said, frowning as she pulled me away.

I shrugged helplessly but indicated I was okay.

"We'll be back," she assured the men.

The long table of champagne flutes, as well as a beautiful champagne fountain, seemed to be a million miles away. However, we did manage to get there in one piece. Gwendolyn was freakishly strong, to be honest.

"Ugh, you work and work and work the circuit and end up being dismissed all the time," she complained, handing me a champagne flute. "Though I've never seen you here before."

"I've never been on the circuit before," I admitted, sipping from my flute. It was very tasty. Then I pulled the glass away from my mouth. "I'm only nineteen," I whispered. "Is someone going to get in trouble?"

She snorted. "Honey, I'm nineteen, too. Trust me, that sort of thing doesn't matter at this level of society."

"Oh." I took another sip. "Thanks for getting me out of there. I really wasn't impressed with that Leopold guy. No offense."

"None taken. I mean, you did hear that he doesn't even know my name, right? I suck his dick, and he calls me every 'G' name under the sun except Gwendolyn. I suppose I should just be grateful he gets the first letter right," she said bitterly.

"I'm sorry. That sucks." I tried to imagine being intimate with someone who couldn't even get my name right.

She looked at me with a sad half-smile. "That's just the way it is. I'm not destitute, but I'm not dripping in diamonds, either. So you just keep going from one to another and hope one decides to keep you as a mistress for a while. Well, maybe not you. Masterson seems to be eager to tie the knot with you. How did you do it?"

"I wasn't even trying," I said, realizing we hadn't gone over our cover story. It wasn't as though I could tell her we'd been chased, kidnapped, and were now being held hostage together. I glanced at Will then decided to just go for it. "He came to the U of M campus, and we met, and things just sort of... grew from there. He really romanced me. Jets. Spain. The whole nine yards. I'm still not sure what he sees in me, but I... I really do love him."

Gwendolyn nodded and sipped her drink. "Makes sense. He went ahead and chose someone lower-class."

I stiffened.

She must have felt it through the arm that was holding me up because she quickly continued. "No, that's not a bad thing! I swear, I'm not insulting you. I mean, it's probably even a good thing. You get a great guy; he gets someone... sincere. Honestly, most of the women here are gold-diggers. Including me." She winked.

"You're just doing what you need to in order to have the life you want," I said. "There's nothing wrong with that. And you seem like a really nice person." I frowned slightly. "Why are you being nice to me?"

"Didn't you see?" she laughed, gesturing to the room with her champagne flute. "We're the two youngest, not upper-class women here. The older harpies are trying to stare us down even as we speak. We're not welcome."

I looked around and noticed that she was right. Women of every age and social standing were staring at us with distaste. Some were subtle. Most were not. "Oh."

"Don't worry. They only work in a few petty jabs when you're with your man. I just wanted to warn you. Girls like us have to stick together," she said.

"Thanks." I glanced back over at Will, who was alternating between talking to Leopold—and a few other pompous old rich guys who had gathered—and looking at me. "Speaking of our men...."

"They won't want us there, anyway. They're discussing business. How about we go sit down? Comunidades en Común didn't do assigned seating tonight, so we can just commandeer a table." She helped me carefully wobble to one of the nearest tables.

I sat down gingerly.

Gwendolyn sat next to me. "This is about to get long and boring. Do you know if Masterson's making a speech? I know his company is one of the top contributors to the organization."

"We honestly have no idea. We just got back, so getting here was kind of done in a rush," I explained. "Will was just wondering if he had to make a speech. I hope he has something prepared, just in case."

"He will. Masterson is always very charming at these things." She sighed. "You are so lucky, McKenzie."

There was no arguing that. "I feel very lucky."

"I leave you alone for two seconds and already you're leaving me for another woman." The boisterous Leopold interrupted our conversation.

We both looked up, Gwendolyn pasting a vapid, yet besotted, expression on her face, me trying to appear at least mildly polite. "Leo, darling!"

Leopold winked at us. "It wouldn't be so bad watching the two of you go at it, though. Am I right, Will?"

Will joined us and frowned at him. "I'd really rather that not happen, actually. Call me old school, but I like it when my fiancée only has eyes for me." He put his hands on my shoulders and kissed the top of my head.

"Just a joke, Will. Just a joke. My, but she does have you by the balls." Leopold laughed.

Will ground his teeth but didn't say anything, sitting down next to me instead. "Is everything all right?" he whispered in my ear.

"Yes. Gwendolyn's lovely. Leopold doesn't deserve her," I whispered back.

He snorted. "Leopold doesn't deserve a goldfish."

Leopold sat down next to her and immediately started getting handsy, trying to get her to put her hand down his pants under the table.

It really grossed me out.

"Are you giving a speech today?" I asked Will, deciding the best thing to do was to ignore the situation.

With a wince, he nodded. "I found out just a few moments ago."

"Do you know what you're going to say?" I fretted on his behalf.

"I'll think of something," he assured me, taking my hand and kissing it. "I've been doing this kind of thing for a while now. I'm in my wheelhouse."

I smiled at him. I was about to say something more when a woman in a long red dress, slit up to the hip, came sashaying over.

"Will," she purred, putting her matching red talons on his shoulder. "It's been forever! Why haven't you called me? I heard you've been back in town for a few days now."

His eyes narrowed, and he gently but firmly, flicked her hand off his shoulder. "Lisa. It's been over a month. And I think you know I'm engaged."

"To this little thing? Well, I wouldn't say 'little.' I didn't know they made couture in your size," Lisa insulted me pleasantly.

I knew I was a bit curvy but hardly overweight. I managed a tight smile. "It's nice to meet you, Lisa. I'm McKenzie." I politely held out my hand for her to shake.

She looked at it as though I'd offered her a dead rat. "Hm. Yes. Will, darling, when you're done playing with this one, you'll remember to call me first, right? I'm the best of all the girls."

"I won't be calling you ever again, Lisa." He was firm, and losing his patience.

She trilled a laugh. "Of course you will, darling. No one can suck you off like I can." She made eye contact with me. "No one."

"Good thing I'm eager to learn, then," I replied sweetly. "Will, *darling* I'm really starting to understand why you left all your friends to come find me."

He smiled and gave me a soft kiss on the temple. "They are rather insufferable, aren't they?"

Lisa gave an indignant squeal, but we ignored her.

Will took my hand. "You're the most beautiful woman I've ever met, McKenzie. Sweet, kind, funny, and authentic. I love you very much."

Conversation at the table came to a halt.

"I love you, too," I said into the silence.

"Will, you can't possibly—!" Lisa protested.

"Lisa, I say this with as much grace as I can muster. Get lost," he responded coldly.

She spluttered and turned then picked up a champagne flute. "I have never been so insulted!"

There was no doubt in my mind my beautiful dress was about to be doused. I held my breath as she glared murder at me and tossed the contents....

... onto Will, who had quickly moved to protect me.

FIFTEEN

ROSES AND CHAMPAGNE

Will

Cold champagne soaked through my shirt.

Lisa stared at me, openmouthed, holding the empty flute in her hand. "Will...."

"Are you finished?" I asked, taking the napkin Leopold passed to me and dabbing my suit.

"I didn't mean to—"

"Get me? Oh, I know you didn't. You meant to get my fiancée. I have to tell you, that was completely uncalled for and unacceptable. Now, if you're finished making a scene, I'd appreciate it if you'd go somewhere else. Anywhere else. And never bother me or my fiancée again," I said tightly.

She opened and closed her mouth a few times then blessedly wandered off.

I sighed. "I'm sorry, McKenzie. I wasn't expecting that."

"That's okay. Thanks for getting in the way," she replied, taking the napkin from me and doing some dabbing herself. She gave me an impish grin. "You must be hard to get over."

"I guess so." I put my hand over hers. "I didn't expect that she'd feel so free to disrespect you. That was... bizarre."

She shrugged. "I mean, the whole scene was bizarre, but I'm not really surprised by the disrespect thing. Gwendolyn and I are the youngest not-upper-crust women here. We're bound to catch a little flak."

"That doesn't make it okay," I insisted, feeling indignant. Even on Gwendolyn's behalf.

"No, it doesn't," McKenzie agreed. "But I think I'm going to like people like Lisa better than the ones who use their smiles to hide their contempt and then gossip about me behind my back later."

She had a point. "Still, you're my fiancée. Whether we've had the official party or not doesn't matter. People should be showing you the same respect they show me."

"Maybe they only show respect to your face, too," she suggested with a grin.

I laughed. "The thought has occurred to me on more than one occasion." I decided I was dry enough and took the napkin from her, setting it aside.

The people around us were still pointing and whispering. Lisa was nowhere to be seen.

"Leopold, did you see where Lisa went?" I asked the man who was still trying to get a hand job under the table while we waited for the programming to begin.

He barely looked up. "Security saw her out," he said in a strained grunt.

Gwendolyn must have given in, then. I tried not to be disgusted. Leopold had always been this way.

"That's good, then. No more champagne incidents tonight." I forced a laugh.

"No—ngh—none of those," he responded, beginning to sweat.

McKenzie started frowning, and I squeezed her hand.

"Let's make the rounds for a bit, shall we?" I suggested, taking her hand and pulling her out of her chair.

Once I had her tucked firmly into my arm, and we were a few yards away from the table, she whispered to me, "He's making her do it right there at the table!"

"Yes," I acknowledged, equally put off. "But we're not going to draw attention to it, and I didn't think you wanted to be there for the whole show."

"God no." She shuddered. "It's just... gross. And really mean to Gwendolyn."

"Leopold doesn't care about anyone but Leopold." I sighed. "Don't worry too much about it. Gwendolyn knows that about him by now."

Then she was scowling at me. "So, just because she *knows* he's a creep means she deserve to be treated this way?"

Shit. I walked right into that one. "Well, honeybee...."

"Don't try to soften me up with 'honeybee.' I want to know what you're trying to tell me," she snapped.

"It's just that... Gwendolyn is one of those kinds of girls... who...." I could tell from her expression I was digging my grave deeper with every word. *How to explain?*

"One of those kinds of girls who deserves to have an old creeper make her jerk him off at a big charity event like he was paying her to do it in a back alley somewhere?" she asked.

I was not quite stupid enough to dive into that trap. Or so I thought. "It's not *exactly* like that. But he is kind of paying her, yes."

McKenzie's neck reeled back like she was going to coil up and bite me. "You did *not* just say that out loud!"

"Honeybee," I tried again, "some girls are in it for the money. Cars. Furs. Jewels. Fancy apartments. It's a whole lifestyle. Gwendolyn knows the deal, I promise."

She gave me a shove, tearing away from my arm. She only made it three unfortunate steps until I had to catch her, however.

"Let go of me," she hissed.

"Do you want to fall flat on your face?" I asked.

McKenzie paused then sighed in defeat. "No."

"Trouble in paradise?" a familiar voice asked.

Fuck me sideways. I secured McKenzie on my arm again then turned with my best smile plastered on my face. "Bran Lockwood! I was hoping I'd see you tonight."

At a champagne only event, Bran had somehow managed to get himself a tumbler of scotch. This did not surprise me in the slightest.

"Will Masterson. As I live and breathe. And this must be McKenzie?" he asked, smiling at her in a way that made me want to smack it right off his face.

"Y-Yes." She recovered herself and beamed back at him, extending her hand for him to shake. "I'm McKenzie Kent."

"A pleasure." The asshole kissed her hand.

I gritted my teeth but kept my composure. "McKenzie and I were just—"

"It's so silly. I have a terrible time with these heels, you see." She jumped in, still smiling at that snake. "But I *insisted* on Will letting me walk around on my own and, well, you saw what happened."

"Yes, I don't know how you women do it," Bran oozed back, still holding her hand.

With a little laugh, she subtly snatched her hand back. "I don't either. I guess I'm just a country girl at heart."

"That's sweet." His eyes raked over her body, and I had to resist the urge to punch him when he lingered a little too long on certain assets. "My, my, they do grow them nicely out in dairyland."

Her cheeks flushed. "Um... thank you?"

"Oh, that was definitely a compliment. Now that I've seen you, I can see why Will decided he needed to snap you up. If I'd met you first...." He let the speculation hang in the air.

"It's been great seeing you, Bran. All the best to the family," I said sweetly, starting to tug her away.

He gripped my other arm. "What's your hurry? Afraid I'll steal her away from you?"

McKenzie looked up at me with concern, but I just smiled down at her—my fake smile, which I knew she was beginning to understand—and patted her hand. "It seems Bran wants to spend a little more time getting to know you, my darling."

"Don't you mean 'honeybee'?" he asked smugly.

Her face lost all color, and my heart slammed hard against my chest. "What did you say?" I asked.

"It's just that you were calling her that a minute ago when you were fighting about Gwendolyn," he smirked.

This motherfucker! "I didn't realize you were close enough to hear that." I tried not to seethe.

McKenzie's cheeks flushed. "It was a stupid argument."

"I agree," Bran said sympathetically. "Leopold Cross is a 'creeper' and Gwendolyn does deserve better. But she's young and relatively new to the circuit. It takes a while to work your way up." He chuckled. "Unless you're a cute little college farm girl, I guess."

She blinked, and I made a fist at my side. "Do you have something you're trying to say, Bran?" I asked, seething for real now.

"I'm just surprised, that's all. I'm not trying to be insulting. I'm really impressed. A girl with no discernible smidgen of breeding has completely swept you off your feet—so much so that you're struggling not to punch me right now. Yet, she's not your usual type at all. You like them your age or even a bit older. Refined. Jaded, even. Women who know the deal, such as Gwendolyn. Well, maybe not Gwendolyn. She's far too young for you." He sized up McKenzie once more. "She's beautiful, granted. And smart. And sassy. I'd definitely keep her around for at least a year if she were mine. But marry her? Honestly, your grandfather must be spitting tacks!"

"He can spit whole steel rods for all I care. Now that you've had your say and been truly insulting, would it be all right if we found someone more pleasant to speak to?" I asked icily.

Bran, being Bran, just burst out laughing. "Now, now, don't get all prickly. I was simply pointing out the obvious. You know everybody's talking about it—and I do mean everybody. How did she do it?"

I opened my mouth to say something regrettable, which was exactly what he was hoping for—to get a rise out of me.

McKenzie beat me to the punch. "Actually, it's because I suck dick better than anyone on this planet, old or young," she said sweetly.

I choked.

He paused, then howled with laughter. "Well, I wasn't expecting that!" He doubled over and held his knee with the hand that wasn't holding his drink. "Oh, I like her. Come by the house Saturday. I'm having a pool party. I'll even invite Gwendolyn."

"We... might not be free," I managed, still trying to wrap my head around what she had just said.

"I'm sure your assistant can move some things around." He said it in a tone that brooked no argument. "After all, wouldn't your grandfather be pleased as punch at you for keeping good relations with Bran Lockwood... the Fifth?"

"So... you're a fifth and that makes you better than a third?" McKenzie asked, sounding unimpressed.

I wanted to kiss her. And warn her not to say the sucking dick thing again while we were here. But mostly kiss her.

"It does, as a matter of fact," he chuckled. "But I appreciate the loyalty. You really do have something special there, Will. I hope you manage to keep her."

"He won't have any problems there." She smiled up at me—a genuine, loving smile—even though we were technically still fighting.

"Aw. That's sweet. I'll let you get back to fighting about Gwendolyn. See you Saturday." Bran grinned. He raised his glass to us, took a sip, then wandered off to find a new victim.

I smiled down at McKenzie and kissed her nose. "I don't want to make a mess of your make-up."

She sniffed. "I'm still mad at you."

"I know."

"You should apologize to Gwendolyn for ever thinking that way about her," she continued.

I sighed. "I don't think any way about her, honeybee. I'm just telling you how the game is played. Hopefully, she'll be able to trade up soon."

"You make it all sound so... transactional," she muttered.

"It... sort of is," I said.

Her shoulders drooped. "I don't like it."

There were a few things I knew I could say. But mostly, I wanted to be as honest as I could be. "McKenzie, as someone who has bene-fitted from the system, I have to say that I, personally, always treated —treat—women with respect. What you need to realize, however, is that a lot of the power rests with them. They can choose to leave, or trade up, or whatever they want to do whenever they want. Bran's taken more than a few of my companions. Mostly because he's an asshole. I've... never wanted anything serious, so I've only had two serious partners, and those only because Grandfather insisted. I've never thought about being anything but a bachelor before, and I found the way things work to be... convenient. But everything changed for me when I met you." I carefully stroked her hair, not wanting to muss it. "So, yes, I'm one of *those* assholes. And I'm hoping you love me anyway."

She bit her lip. "Of course, I love you anyway. What do they say? 'Don't hate the player, hate the game'?"

I laughed and pulled her into a hug. "Thanks."

"Thank you for being honest," she replied.

"Always." I kissed her hair.

"And for helping me find something or someone better for Gwendolyn," she said.

I groaned. "I knew it was going to cost me."

"But you will?"

"I will," I agreed. "You're right. She deserves better."

"Good." She leaned up and kissed my cheek.

I was sure she'd left a lipstick mark, but I didn't care.

I was hers, after all.

SIXTEEN

HYPOCRITICAL SPEECHES

McKenzie

Before I could find a napkin to get my lipstick off his cheek, an older Hispanic man in a suit came rushing up to us. "Mr. Masterson! Thank goodness. We'd like to kick off the proceedings now, and I thought you could give your speech pre-dinner. You're always so good at introducing the organization and our mission, and Fernando, sadly, just came down with the flu. He's heading out the door even as we speak."

"Mr. Nieves," Will said, putting a hand on his shoulder. "Don't give yourself a heart attack, please. If Mr. Garcia is ill, of course, I'll take his place."

"Thank you." Mr. Nieves looked as though he might cry with relief. "We had it all so planned out. I was just so worried no one would be able to fill in for him. You know how awful I am at speeches."

Will smiled. "Yes, but you have many other wonderful qualities, Mr. Nieves. Now, let me just get my fiancée back to our table, and I'll be right with you."

The organizer nodded. "Oh... you have a smudge on your cheek, Mr. Masterson."

Will grinned down at me. "I kind of thought so."

"Would you like me to get a wet napkin?" Mr. Nieves asked.

With a shake of his head, Will said, "I actually rather like it right where it is."

"Oh. Yes, of course." Mr. Nieves smiled at me. "You are a very lucky young lady."

"I know," I replied. "And I would love to hear more about Comunidades en Común later."

"Please, sit with us. Keep McKenzie company while I'm giving my speech," Will said.

I smiled. This person, at least, seemed to be sincere. A man who was exactly what he appeared to be. "I'd like that very much."

"Really?" Mr. Nieves puffed up a bit. "I will happily keep you company, Miss...?"

"Kent," I provided. "McKenzie Kent."

"Miss Kent. I am Mr. Alonso Nieves. I'm so pleased to meet you." He shook my hand with both of his.

"I'm pleased to meet you as well." *See, Ike? I can be perfectly polite. Suck it!*

Will escorted me back to the table with Mr. Nieves trotting beside us. Once I was seated, Will kissed my forehead. "Don't let Mr. Nieves steal your heart away while I'm gone."

Mr. Nieves laughed. "As though I could at my age!"

"Are you sure you want to go up there with my lipstick on your cheek?" I asked.

"Absolutely. Now, if you'll excuse me." Will nodded to Mr. Nieves, Leopold, Gwendolyn....

... and Bran, who decided to join our table. "Looks like there's a free spot."

Will's expression soured as Bran settled a buxom blonde in hot pink in one of the chairs then took the last one.

"Her name is Sheila." Bran winked at me. "Oh look, no more chairs for Will. Pity."

"Mr. Lockwood! It's such an honor," Mr. Nieves said quickly. "Please, don't worry. I will be doing my duties as host. I'm only saving Mr. Masterson's chair until he is finished giving his speech."

At the mention of his speech, Will went to do his duty, glancing back at me several times.

"Really? What happened to Mr. Garcia?" Bran asked with what I could tell was false concern.

"He has taken ill," Mr. Nieves replied. "Poor man."

"Here?" Sheila piped up in a nasal voice. She looked around. "Do you think it's contagious?"

"I'm sure it will be fine, dear," Bran said, waving a hand.

Sheila wrinkled her nose. "I don't want to get sick."

"Mr. Garcia left immediately so as not to expose you," Mr. Nieves assured her.

"If he was sick, he shouldn't have come at all." Sheila sounded quite miffed. "But then, his kind always spreads disease."

A dissonant ringing started in my head. "'His kind'?" I repeated.

Bran was already scowling at Sheila, but she didn't pick up on it.

"You know." Sheila waved in Mr. Nieves' direction. "His kind."

The ringing stopped as something snapped in my head. Mr. Nieves drooped, clearly too polite to correct her, or maybe thinking it wasn't his place.

As the fiancée of William Masterson the Third, and, more importantly, a decent human being, I had no such qualms. "Well, aren't you just a classless, ignorant—"

"I think Sheila was just leaving," Bran said, his voice as cold as ice.

Sheila's head whipped around from me to Bran. "But, darling, didn't you hear what she said about me?!"

"Yes, and I've stopped her before she really lays into you. I apologize, Mr. Nieves. Sheila will not be showing up at any more of your functions—or anywhere on the circuit, for that matter," Bran said.

"What?! What are you talking about?!" Sheila squawked.

Now Leopold and Gwendolyn were paying attention. "I say, dinner *and* a show," Leopold chuckled.

"Sheila, I think our relationship has run its course. You have embarrassed me and done undue damage to my reputation. And I don't ever want to see you again. Anywhere. So take the last hundred thousand dollars I gave you and go prey on the elderly on the west coast." Bran was no less cold. "Do you understand?"

She paled then stood and tossed down her napkin. "I can't believe you're casting me aside for a bunch of wetbacks."

I wished I still had champagne to dump on her. I eyed Bran's scotch.

His lips twitched ever so slightly, and he pulled it back toward him. "Mr. Nieves, would you mind getting security to show Miss James out?"

"It will be my pleasure, Mr. Lockwood." Mr. Nieves stood, and, with his head held high, went to get security.

I didn't believe it was a coincidence when two burly Hispanic gentlemen in all black came wandering back with him, both glaring death at Sheila.

"You've got to be kidding me," she grumbled.

"Bye-bye now," Bran said. "Don't let the door hit you on the way out."

Sheila protested loudly as the two Hispanic security guards took her by each arm and escorted her out. Everyone in the room, which must have been filled with a hundred people, stared.

"Well, that was entertaining," Will said from the podium in front. "On that note, I'd like to welcome you to the twenty-seventh annual dinner for Comunidades en Común."

The audience clapped.

"This really will be something to listen to. Will makes the best speeches," Bran murmured to me as though nothing had happened.

"Oh, quite," Leopold agreed. "It's almost a blessing that Mr. Garcia became ill. He does drone on so."

"I would have liked to have heard his speech, too," I said defensively.

Mr. Nieves smiled at me.

"Probably not." Leopold was oblivious to my censure, apparently.

"As you know," Will continued, putting paid to the conversation, "this organization has been working diligently in Central America for all twenty-seven of those years. What started as a small school in one Honduran village has turned into a multi-country initiative, incorporating healthcare, food support, and housing as pillars upholding the ultimate goal of elevating families out of poverty through education. I wish Fernando was here to tell you about the hard work of the early days, dengue fever, polluted water, and leaky roofs. He was there, boots on the ground, helping with all of it. All of us who are now involved couldn't be more honored to be here tonight, celebrating the twenty-seventh-year milestone that started in one little village."

The audience clapped.

Will winked at the room. "Of course, we're not here to just eat dinner and reminisce about old times. We're also opening our wallets, as well as our hearts, to this great organization that they might continue and even expand their work. Tonight, we have silent auction items which many of you may have already seen and bid on along the tables there." He pointed to the tables lining the walls.

I'd been so preoccupied with the other things happening around me that I hadn't noticed the tables. I wondered if he and I should see what was being auctioned and make some bids. It seemed only polite.

"Dinner will be served in the next fifteen minutes, I'm told," he continued. "Then we will have the main auction event of the bigger items. I'm expecting some enthusiasm here, people."

Everyone laughed.

"Good, now that we have an understanding, let's enjoy some great food, good company, and the great many items we're all about to go bid on." He gave a charming smile, glancing around the room until his eyes fell on me.

I knew immediately it was his fake smile. I tensed with concern.

Will stepped down and came back to the table to a round of applause. Mr. Nieves stood up immediately, still clapping.

"Thank you so much, Mr. Masterson. A great speech, as always," he praised.

"Thank you, Mr. Nieves. It's always an honor and a pleasure." Will sat down next to me and draped an arm around the back of my chair.

I put a hand on Will's thigh while Mr. Nieves excused himself to go coordinate the dinner service. "Will?" I whispered.

He stroked the back of my neck. "It's okay, honeybee. We'll talk about it later."

When we were alone, no doubt. Still, as they laid plates in front of us, I could tell he was really disturbed. He didn't touch his food.

"That's quite the stamp you have on your cheek, Will," Bran teased from across the table.

Will nodded, absently pushing pieces of steak around his plate.

"You know what," I said, standing. "I might need to powder my nose. Will? Would you like to show me where to go?"

He glanced up at me then nodded. "How remiss of me. I'll take you there." He offered me his arm, and we walked away.

I could just hear Bran behind us, chuckling to Leopold. "You know they're not going to the powder room, right? Somebody's about to get lucky."

Leopold chortled right back.

I decided to ignore them and hoped Will would, too. If he did overhear them, he didn't show it.

"What's wrong?" I asked once we left the main hall. "You seem really upset."

He paused, then tugged me away from where the bathrooms were clearly labeled with brass plates. We walked across the marble floor to a different room, one that was laid out as though it could host a very small wedding reception.

Will didn't turn on the lights. He just lifted me and sat me on the edge of a table.

Was he hoping to get lucky? "Uh… Will.…"

He wrapped his arms around me and dropped his head on my shoulder. "I just gave a speech about elevating children out of poverty, knowing full well we're kidnapping those same children and selling them into slavery. I feel like such a hypocrite. Hell, I feel like I need a shower."

"Oh. Yeah, I guess I would, too," I responded after thinking it over. I ran my fingers through his hair, wondering what I could possibly do to comfort him. "You're not like Ike. You're never going to be like him."

"Grandfather wants me to be. He's going to make me do this dance until he breaks me," he sighed.

I clutched his head, my fingers tangled in his hair. "He's not going to break you. We're getting out, remember?"

Will paused far too long for my liking, so I kicked him in the shin.

"Ouch!" He winced. "McKenzie!"

"And let that be a lesson to you," I told him. "If you keep giving up hope, next time, this heel is going to go right in your balls!"

He laughed and hugged me tighter. "Okay, okay. I was having some pretty dark thoughts, but as usual, you knew just what to do to drag me out of it."

"Exactly." I stroked his hair again.

After a long silence, he said, "We will get out. Together."

SEVENTEEN

A LITTLE BIT OF COMFORT

Will

As I said the words, I was surprised to find that, not only did I mean them, but I also believed them.

McKenzie sagged against me, and I heard her sniffle.

"Honeybee, you're going to ruin your make-up," I said, pushing her back a bit. I took a handkerchief from my pocket and handed it to her.

She very carefully dabbed her eyes, getting only a little bit of mascara on the handkerchief. "Crap."

"It's fine. You can't even notice," I reassured her.

"I've just... been so worried about you," she choked out. She cleared her throat. "It seemed like you were giving up."

I winced. "I had a moment. I'm sorry."

McKenzie touched my cheek. "We all have our moments. Just don't let it happen too often, okay? My heart can't take it."

"Hey," I grinned. "I'm the old fart here. It's *my* heart that's going to give out if anyone's heart is giving out on us."

She snorted. "Old fart my ass. I feel like I need to be getting in more cardio every time we have sex!"

I wiggled my eyebrows at her. "I can't think of a better way to get in your cardio. Sure beats counting steps."

McKenzie swatted me. "Not the point." She reversed my hand-kerchief and found a clean spot, then licked it slowly.

Suddenly, I had new ideas regarding cardio. "What... exactly are you doing?"

"Getting the lipstick off your cheek, what do you think?" She wiped my cheek carefully with the handkerchief.

All I could see was her tongue slowly licking the cloth, and I stifled a groan. While I'd heard what Bran and Leopold had said as we left the hall, and been disgusted at the time, the horny teenager who had come to rest inside me ever since meeting McKenzie was now jumping up and down for attention.

"Maybe we should get back," I wheezed, wondering if tonight was, indeed, the night I would finally have a heart attack. I was going to have to sit through the entire auction lusting after her and not be able to have her, after all.

"Do we have to? Those people are really unpleasant. No offense," she said, making a face.

I chuckled. "Yes, they really are. And we're going to be spending a lot more time with them at this and that function."

She groaned. "Oh my God, being rich is *torture*. How do you put up with it all?"

"Simple. I have you." This time, I kissed her lips, not caring about her lipstick anymore.

McKenzie squeaked. "But I just finished cleaning you off!"

"Tough. I'm not going to make it through the rest of the night without a little honey." I kissed her again.

She laughed then stopped laughing when I kissed my way down her neck. "Will... can we really do it here?"

I hadn't been planning to go all the way, but I was a starving man. I needed her. Desperately. "Please, say yes." I knew I was begging. I didn't care.

"But I mean... logistically...?" She tugged at her dress.

I bent down and smoothed her skirt all the way up to her waist. "Logistics handled."

McKenzie swallowed then took the skirt from my hands and held it up herself. "You can't tear these panties while we're here."

"But I can tear them later?" I asked hopefully, working the small swatch of fabric between her legs aside.

"Well, I know you're going to tear them later. I'm not a complete moron. I'm just saying we're going to need them to protect the dress while we're here," she said. "I don't want to look like I peed myself."

"Tearing them later. Got it." I kissed her again, pushing two fingers inside her.

She moaned, her tight body getting wet almost immediately.

"Ready for me already?" I murmured in her ear. "Were you thinking about it, too?"

McKenzie nodded. "Ever since Bran said something."

"Let's not ever say his name again during sex. Deal?" I replied, frowning.

"Deal," she said. She widened her knees for me.

I didn't need a second invitation. I opened my pants and tugged her to the edge of the table, sheathing my rigid cock inside her.

We both groaned as she stretched to accommodate me.

"Put your arms around me. I've got the dress," I managed between my teeth as I took the fabric and held onto it, and her hips, and started to thrust.

She whimpered and wrapped her arms around my neck, burying her face there to muffle the noises she made.

I grunted, thrusting myself in her tight, wet heat over and over again.

"D-Don't get the dress dirty!" she said through chattering teeth.

I chuckled. I could tell she was close. "We'll do our best, won't we, honeybee?" I rubbed my thumb over her clit.

"Mm!" She just managed to press her mouth into my skin before crying out her climax. She even gave me a little bite!

"That was naughty." My orgasm hit me right in the back of the head, traveling up my spine from where we were joined. I came hard inside her, crushing my lips to hers to stop my own bellow.

We stayed there, panting, for a long moment. I would have been perfectly happy to go again or go home and forget the whole fucking event.

"We have to go back." She interrupted my thoughts. "And be careful pulling out. We don't want to get the dress."

"I'd rather just go home and rip the panties." I knew I sounded petulant.

McKenzie laughed and kissed me. "Me, too. But we're being good for now, right?"

I thought of Ike, and then my grandfather, finding out we'd ditched the charity event. They might not say anything, but she was right. It would not be a point in our favor. "We're being good," I agreed grumpily.

"Here." She handed me back her handkerchief. "Make sure we don't get the dress."

"You really like this dress, don't you?" I teased, pulling out very carefully and cleaning us both up.

She shrugged. "It's a nice dress. Probably the nicest thing I've ever worn."

"There will be a hundred other dresses just as stylish and pretty," I told her. "But, if you really like this one, I promise not to rip it off you when we get home."

McKenzie rubbed the back of her neck as I got her underwear back in place and tugged her skirt down. "All this money is kind of a weird concept to me. I was sort of shooting for a middle-class kind of life, you know? Like most people. Your world is... yeah...."

"'Yeah'?" I asked.

"Don't tell me you're jumping on team Ike about that." She pouted.

"No, I mean, what about my world is 'yeah'?" I asked.

She gestured around us in the near-dark of the small reception hall. "Just... it's a lot. And I feel like I've only seen the tip of the iceberg."

I gave her a chaste kiss and helped her down off the table. She wobbled even more on her heels, and I wasn't sure whether to be proud of my prowess or chagrined that I'd made it even harder for her to walk. "It's our world, for now. Honestly, I'd happily live in a cardboard box as long as I had you."

"Would you like some wine with your cheese?" she laughed.

I laughed, too, while she took my arm. "I mean it, though."

"I know." She leaned up and kissed my cheek, causing her to crash against me.

"Let's get you seated, shall we?" I chuckled, tossing the handker-chief in the trash. I held her up as we left the small reception room and headed back toward the main hall.

Gwendolyn was just coming out. She took one look and stopped us. "Oh no you don't. You're not going back in there looking like *that*. Both of you need to go to the powder room. ASAP." Her eyes narrowed on me. "Your own powder room."

"Do we look that bad?" McKenzie asked, patting her hair.

"Let's just say everyone will know what you were doing. Come on, I'll take you. It doesn't look like you brought a clutch, so I'm assuming you didn't bring any extra make-up to repair the damage?" Gwendolyn inferred.

"Er... no," McKenzie mumbled.

Gwendolyn shrugged. "All right. We'll be using mine. Mr. Masterson, we'll see you in a bit." She strong-armed McKenzie off me and supported her to the ladies' room.

It was the first time I noticed McKenzie's make-up was actually smeared. I'd been so busy imagining what we might do to pass the time in a cardboard box that all I saw was my beautiful honeybee and not the damage I'd done.

With a sigh, I headed to the men's room.

I was somehow not surprised to see Bran there. He took one look at me and laughed. "I didn't know you had such a wildcat! I'll have to visit the U of M one of these days. Looks like it's Girls Gone Wild over there!"

"Ha-ha." I looked in the mirror and winced. *Good thing Gwendolyn stopped us.* I was sporting McKenzie's lipstick on my face and neck. It must have all rubbed off her because it faded more and more as the marks continued.

There was even some on the collar of my shirt. I took a paper towel from the carefully placed dishes on the counter, ran it under the faucet, and got to work.

"My friend, that's lipstick. The only way you're getting that off your shirt is if you send it to the dry cleaner," Bran chuckled.

I rubbed at the stain until it was a faint pink then grunted in frustration when, as he said, it wouldn't come out any more than that. No matter how hard I tried.

"Don't worry about it. I think people will be more distracted by that bite you've got on your neck. Rawr!" He continued to laugh.

"Please refrain from harassing McKenzie when we get back to the table. This was all my fault, and I don't want her embarrassed because of it," I said, frowning at him.

He held up his hands. "I won't say a word. Maybe a few words. All right, I am going to rib you mercilessly, but I'll leave her out of it. Mostly."

I groaned. "Bran, please."

"I tell you what. You promise to show up at my pool party Saturday, and I'll even shut down Leopold for you," he bargained.

With a sigh, I agreed. "Deal."

"Excellent! She must have a great natural complexion. I'd have expected to see some more foundation on your jacket." He grinned.

I looked in the mirror again and swore. "You've got to be kidding me!"

"That's why you only get blowjobs at these things. Then you only need to worry about make-up in places you can cover with your jacket," he advised me.

"You sound like an authority on the subject," I said, not sure whether to use water or not to try to get the foundation off me.

Bran reached into his pocket and tossed me a small bottle. "Make-up remover. Dab, don't rub. Since Sheila's not here, I'm not going to need it. Works on all clothes. Then get it to the dry cleaner when you get home. And yes, I am an authority on the subject."

I blinked at the bottle in my hand.

"You can thank me by bringing McKenzie in a bikini. It's rare to see a homegrown hourglass figure these days." He winked at me then quickly exited the bathroom.

A wise decision on his part.

EIGHTEEN
MAKE-UP

McKenzie

"At least you didn't get the dress," Gwendolyn clucked, her clutch opening to reveal an all-occasion fix-it kit.

I didn't know if I was more impressed at its contents or that it all fit in her little purse. "We were very careful," I said.

She raised an eyebrow at me and gestured to the mirror where I could see my make-up was smeared, and my hair was coming out of its pins. "Yes, very careful," she deadpanned.

I blushed. "Thanks for saving me."

"Like I said, we need to help each other. Though, I am surprised Mr. Masterson did something like this during a charity event. That's not his thing. Or maybe it is now." She eyed me speculatively. "You're kind of a game changer."

"Without trying to be. I don't know. He was a little sad and... things just kind of... evolved from there," I said. "It wasn't exactly planned."

Gwendolyn turned me so she could get to work on my face. "Sad about what? He gave a great speech."

"I know. It's... complicated." I wished there was someone I could talk to about the situation. But I didn't know her that well, and Will and I were on dangerous ground as it was.

"Is he worried that he's thirty and you're nineteen? You've got to get thoughts like that out of his head as soon as he has them. If that was the issue, I would have fucked him six ways to Sunday, too." She carefully used make-up remover on my light foundation. "You have great skin. Don't bother with foundation next time. Especially if you're going to end up cheering him up again."

"Thanks," I replied. "And, really, thank you, Gwendolyn. And yeah, sometimes he's worried that I'm nineteen, and he's thirty. As if that matters!"

"Boys are dumb," she said sagely. "He's handsome, cultured, probably excellent in bed, and he has money. Lots of money. You'd think they'd have nothing to feel insecure about." She paused. "But, always have an exit strategy. And keep your body up. He's got all that on his side, but we've just got youth, charm, and rocking good blowjobs on ours."

My old insecurities surfaced. Even though I knew I shouldn't, I still sometimes wondered what he saw in me. "He's planning to marry me."

"I know. I have three words for you: prenup, prenup, prenup! When another nineteen-year-old comes along when you're in your late twenties or early thirties, you want to make sure you're provided for," she said. "Unless you're planning to go back to dairyland."

"I'm actually planning to finish college. I don't want anything but love from him." I winced when she poked me in the eye with the mascara wand.

Instead of apologizing, she gave me a little shake. "Snap out of it! I know you're blissfully happy now, but eventually, you're going to get used to this lifestyle. Whatever you were studying in college is not going to get you what you have now. If you want to keep it, prenup. Besides, if you want to work in your field after being the wifey for ten or fifteen years, who's going to hire you for an entry-level position? Ageism is a thing."

"But—"

"No buts. Prenup." She went back to doing my make-up.

My shoulders sagged, and I felt a bit defeated.

"And straighten your posture," she added.

I had to laugh and did straighten up. "Has Bran asked you to his Saturday pool party yet?"

"I was going to meet him in the men's room to discuss it—and probably blow him—but this seemed more important," she grinned.

"Oh no!" I realized I'd cost her an opportunity to trade up. Way up. "I'm sorry."

"Don't worry about it. I've caught his attention now, and it's not like we could have done a lot with Mr. Masterson in there. Besides, I think I intrigue him because of you, and that's something to be thankful for," she said.

I blinked. "Because of me?"

Gwendolyn nodded. "Yes. Now, no talking, I'm putting on your lipstick."

"But—"

"Shh." She carefully applied the lipstick. "You're my friend now. And he wants to get into your pants. So he's going to try to do that through me. I doubt it'll work, and when he figures that out, I'll be yesterday's news. But, in the meantime, I'll get to have some fun and hopefully get some money I can put away for a rainy day."

When she was finished with my lipstick, I asked, "He thinks he's getting in *my* pants?!"

"He's jealous of Mr. Masterson, of course. It's well-known on the circuit that Mr. Lockwood is always going after Mr. Masterson's conquests. Wants to prove he's better, I suppose. I just... don't think he's going to be successful this time." She winked at me. "You're too far gone for that to happen."

"Does... Bran know that you know his plans?" I asked.

Gwendolyn laughed. "Like I said. Boys are dumb. He doesn't think women have two brain cells to rub together, much less catch on to what he's thinking. But my mama didn't raise no fool."

"You should be a millionaire," I said, impressed.

"Well, with any luck, I will be one day." She turned me to look in the mirror. "Not bad if I do say so myself. I'm just going to adjust the pins in your hair, and then we'll be ready to go."

"Thank you again. Really." I was truly impressed with her work.

She patted my shoulder. "No, thank you. I was never going to land Mr. Lockwood without your help."

"What are you going to do about Leopold?" I asked, curious.

"Don't worry. He already has eyes on Natalie Grace. She's *eighteen*, you know." She rolled her eyes. "Who knew nineteen was the new sixty?"

I laughed, yet sort of felt bad for Natalie. "Who knew?"

We walked back to the hall together with me hanging on Gwendolyn's arm. As she suspected, Leopold was already chatting up a raven-haired, thin young beauty who was now occupying Gwendolyn's chair.

Bran patted the one next to him. "Come on over here, Gwennie. Looks like you've been displaced, to my good fortune."

'Gwennie' giggled and went over to Bran after depositing me back next to Will.

"Seems there's been a change in the game," Will whispered, looking around the table.

"Yeah, a happy one, too," I said. "Gwendolyn's trading up. Leopold's getting a younger model. Everybody's happy."

"Younger model? Lord, pretty soon he'll be taking them from the cradle," Will muttered.

"I had the same thought." I almost leaned on him but then thought better of it. Make-up.

"I think, next time, you should forget about foundation. Then we can be closer." He voiced my thoughts, holding my hand instead.

Still, I had to tease him. "Maybe I shouldn't wear underwear, either."

He chuckled. "Maybe not. But you know that's not what I was

talking about." He softly kissed my neck. "Now, you tell me what's gotten you out of sorts, and I'll tell you what I bid on for us."

"You bid already?!" I gaped. "When did you do that?"

"I hoped you wouldn't mind. You took longer to get ready than me." He squeezed my hand. "If you want to make the rounds with me—"

I thought of my wobbly legs and shook my head vehemently. "I'm sure you found some lovely things to bid on."

Will smiled. "I did. The auction of the larger items is starting soon, but don't try to get me sidetracked. Something you talked about in there made you uncomfortable."

The man was psychic. How did he always know these things?! "I was talking to Gwendolyn...."

"That's a given." He gave me an expectant look.

"And... she just happened to mention... a lot of things about securing my future since... um...." I didn't quite know how to tell him without upsetting him.

He raised an eyebrow. "I'm not going to like this, am I?"

"Probably not," I mumbled.

"Are you losing your confidence in us again?" He sounded disappointed.

I did exactly what Gwendolyn told me not to. I hunched my shoulders. "Well, she was just saying how people like her and I don't exactly have... a lot more to offer... than being... pretty."

Will groaned. "I knew this wasn't going anywhere good."

"I can't help it. I get insecure sometimes," I defended myself. "It just... it doesn't always make sense why you're into me. I mean, Bran was just talking about—"

"What was I talking about?" Bran asked from across the table.

The man had ears like a bat! "Um... nothing," I said quickly.

"I was just about to find out why you're a bigger asshole than I already thought," Will returned without missing a beat.

Bran burst out laughing. "I'd love to know why I'm at the center of your little spat. It looks as though you're gearing up for a good one."

"I think it's probably the comment you made about McKenzie not being my usual type," Will replied, his expression daring me to contradict him.

I winced. He wasn't wrong. "I'm sure he was just making an observation." *Wait, why am I defending the asshole who wants to get in my pants?!*

"Uh-huh. No, darling—" Will began.

"Honeybee," Bran corrected him with a smirk.

Will glared death at him. "Bran's just being a world-class jerk. He was trying to poke holes in your confidence."

Bran put a hand to his chest, his jaw dropping theatrically. "Who, me?"

"Yes, you." Will squeezed my hand. "You have nothing to worry about. No one compares to you. No one ever has. No one ever will."

"And just in case, get a prenup." Bran grinned.

I groaned. "Why does everyone want me to get a prenup?"

"Because it's the smart thing to do," Bran replied logically. "That way, when Will realizes he misses his older, sophisticated women—"

"You're going to want to stop yourself right there," Will growled.

Bran held up his hands. "All right. But don't say I didn't warn you."

"If we get a prenup, it's going to say McKenzie gets my whole fortune in the event of a divorce," Will said. "End of discussion."

I stared at him. "What?!"

"End. Of. Discussion," Will repeated.

Even Bran looked taken aback. "Wow. That's putting a lot of faith in a nineteen-year-old country girl."

"I have a lot of faith in my nineteen-year-old country girl," Will replied. "And as for you...."

"Ladies and gentlemen," Mr. Nieves said from the podium, preventing Will from completing his thought. "It is now time for the auction. Bidding is closed on the silent auction, and winners will be announced at the end."

Excited murmurs filled the room.

"Now, our first item is a weekend retreat at the Masterson vacation home on Lake Geneva..." Mr. Nieves said.

I had a very bad feeling.

"...with Mr. Masterson and his lovely fiancée McKenzie Kent..."

"Ike is a dead man," Will grunted.

Bran was grinning.

This was very, very bad.

NINETEEN

GOING ONCE, GOING TWICE

Will

That asshole was going to bid.

"Bran, don't," I growled.

I shouldn't have said it. It just made his grin wider.

"I think it will be a lovely weekend. I'll even bring Gwennie," he mused, petting her arm.

Gwendolyn giggled.

"Who's Gwennie?" Leopold asked, confused.

I sighed and pointed to her.

"Right. Greta." He turned back to Natalie with an unbothered smile.

"It's fine," McKenzie whispered, touching my thigh. "It could be a really nice weekend."

"We're already going to his pool on Saturday," I argued.

"Which will also be great fun." He winked at us and raised his hand to bid. "Fifty thousand."

"Oh! We're starting quite high, then," Mr. Nieves said with a wide smile. "Yes, erm, fifty thousand...."

"Actually, let's call it a hundred and fifty," Bran interrupted, outbidding himself.

Mr. Nieves blinked. "Yes, of course. Yes, thank you, Mr. Lockwood. Do I hear...?"

"On second thought, I think an even million has a nice ring to it, don't you, Will?" Bran teased.

While I ground my teeth, Mr. Nieves fanned himself with a program. "Sounds great, Bran," I said through my teeth.

"I thought so. Yes. Now, is there anyone who would like to bid above me? Poor Mr. Nieves looks as though he may faint," Bran called to the room.

The other patrons laughed good-naturedly.

"Well, just to make sure I'm not outbid, I'll give you ten million, Mr. Nieves. Final bid," Bran offered.

Mr. Nieves did, indeed, look as though he might faint. I wondered if I should get him a chair. "Mr. Lockwood, you are exceedingly generous," he wheezed. "Um... ten million going once, ten million going twice...."

There were no other bids. I knew there wouldn't be.

Mr. Nieves brought down a gavel procured for the occasion. "Sold to Mr. Lockwood for ten million dollars!"

A round of applause thundered through the room.

"Thank you," Bran said, standing and bowing. "I hope this small act encourages everyone else to be just as generous."

The applause continued. Even Mr. Nieves applauded.

And McKenzie, who bumped my shoulder.

Reluctantly, I also clapped.

"Please continue, Mr. Nieves. I'm sure there are many other wonderful items and opportunities on offer," Bran said.

"Yes, yes there are," Mr. Nieves replied and continued.

I didn't hear anything else. All I could concentrate on was Bran's smug smirk.

"Will," McKenzie said after a while, "is there anything you

want? I mean, you don't *have* to bid on anything. I just thought it might... you know... look good."

She was right. It would look good to Ike—and my grandfather. Both of whom I wanted to strangle. "Thank you, darling—"

"Honeybee," Bran corrected me.

Scratch that. Bran had moved to first in line for strangulation. "McKenzie," I amended.

He chuckled and went back to having a whispered conversation with Gwendolyn.

McKenzie frowned at them then leaned very close to my ear, probably hoping he-who-hears-everything wouldn't hear what she had to say. "You know he can't steal me, right?"

I balked. "Not the point."

"What's the point, then?" she asked, confused.

"I'm going to have to sit there and watch him try," I muttered angrily.

She patted my knee. "He'll give up quickly. You'll see."

I wanted to reply, 'He won't, *you'll* see.' But I didn't. Instead, I sighed and turned my attention to the auction.

There were only a few items left, but I did manage to get a new Ferrari I didn't give a fuck about to make Ike and my grandfather happy. I didn't bid ten million on it. I thought about it, knowing it would not only spite them but also give the proverbial finger to Bran. McKenzie had reminded me, however, that we were being good. So I was good and only bid a hundred thousand more than the car was worth.

"Are we actually going to drive that thing?" she asked me, staring at the picture in the brochure that had been laid in front of us. "It's... um...."

"That is the fugliest Ferrari I've ever seen. No wonder someone was trying to get rid of it!" Bran chortled.

I winced. The paint job wasn't great, even though I knew it must be custom. And, for a Ferrari, it did have a bit of an odd shape. I wouldn't have called it 'fugly,' but it wasn't the classic look, either.

"It looks dangerous," McKenzie whispered.

"Dangerous?" I said.

"Dangerous!" Bran laughed. "Haven't you ever been in a real sports car before?"

She blushed. "No, I don't think so."

"Well, you're in for a treat. Once Will gets that atrocious paint job redone, you can really let your hair down," he said. "Though I'd start with one of his other cars. Something you can put the top down on. Maybe that cute blue McLaren of yours."

That did sound fun. I hated that the idea came from him, but it wasn't a bad idea. "That could be... nice."

He laughed again. "No need to pout. It's a great idea. I just got to it first."

"Fine, yes. You win," I conceded. "It's a great idea."

"Bikini worthy?" he asked, glancing at McKenzie.

She looked up at me, confused.

"Don't push your luck," I replied icily.

"Aw, come on. All the other girls will be wearing bikinis. Probably barely-there bikinis," he wheedled. "McKenzie could wear something completely modest by comparison."

"Of course she'll wear a bikini. You don't want her to look like some old lady in a caftan and a sun hat, do you?" Gwendolyn chimed in. "McKenzie, you'd be the only one there in a full suit on Saturday. You're new to society. You want to fit in, don't you?"

Bran smiled like the cat who got the cream, rubbing Gwendolyn's back.

"I... uh... um...." McKenzie stuttered. "I could always bring a sarong?"

"That's the spirit." He finally looked down at the brochure in front of him showing pictures of the Masterson lake home. "My, this is a quaint little place."

Quaint?! I remembered Grandfather telling me he'd shelled out over thirty million for it. It was one of the largest properties on Lake Geneva.

"It's adorable," Bran decided, leafing through. "Let's decide on a weekend, shall we? We do want to get there while it's still summer to enjoy all the activities."

The man had me by the balls and just kept twisting. "I'm sure our assistants can arrange it."

"Nonsense. I know you haven't got a thing going on that can't be rearranged, and neither do I," he argued, flipping to the back of the brochure. "Oh, this is grand! Ike made a list of available dates."

Of course he did. "That's nice."

"Let me just check my schedule. Gwennie, be a dear and get my phone out of my pocket? Left lapel," he said, not setting down the brochure.

Gwendolyn tittered, and, as sensually as I'd ever seen a phone retrieved, pulled Bran's phone from his jacket.

"Thank you, dearest," he smiled and plucked the phone from her fingers. "Let's see here... yes. Three weeks from now will be perfect."

"Perfect," I echoed, trying not to sound petulant.

McKenzie squeezed my hand. "I'm sure we'll have a very nice weekend."

"See, Will? That's the kind of attitude we're looking for," he chuckled.

"Mm," I replied noncommittally.

"He's just allergic to fun." He winked at McKenzie.

"Will is very fun," she responded, squeezing my hand again.

Bran grinned at me. I could feel myself scowling at him. "Maybe he's only fun when I'm not around."

Gwendolyn patted his chest. "I think they might need a break, lover. They're not understanding your jokes."

He inclined his head. "True. They have been under a lot of stress lately."

Wait, what?!

"How does he know that?" McKenzie whispered, her eyes wide.

"What with planning the engagement party and all. Ike told me at our last meeting," Bran continued, smirking at me.

What else had Ike told him at their last meeting? Suddenly, I wondered if Bran's family was involved in the same illegal dealings mine was. "I think we need to talk privately," I said.

"I'll have Armond schedule something with—"

"Now." I stood stiffly, letting go of McKenzie's hand.

"Should I come, too?" McKenzie asked, beginning to rise.

"No," Bran, I, and even Gwendolyn, said together.

"Let the boys talk. It's just going to be confusing business stuff," Gwendolyn told McKenzie.

McKenzie looked up at me.

"I'll be back soon," I promised, patting her shoulder.

Bran nodded to Leopold and Natalie, who were barely paying attention, then gestured for me to precede him out of the hall.

"Tell me if I won anything from the silent auction," he tossed over his shoulder to Gwendolyn.

"Of course!" she answered.

Once outside the hall, I stopped, unsure of where to lead him. I didn't want to have it out in the bathroom where we could be overheard. But I also didn't want to—

"Why don't we just go to the quiet little reception hall where you and McKenzie fucked?" he suggested.

—take him there.

Wait.... "How did you know where we were?" I asked, narrowing my eyes.

"Why don't we talk about it in private?" he said, putting an arm around my shoulders and steering me to the reception room where McKenzie and I had been intimate.

I rounded on him when the door closed behind us. "What the *fuck*, Bran?!"

"Clever. That one sentence covers so many subjects all at once." He grinned at me. "Did you think Ike was just going to let you wander around on your own after your little adventure?"

My blood ran cold. "What?"

"You heard me. Honestly, I always thought you were a little

dense, but not so naïve as to not know how many of us do business. Especially your own grandfather—at the company you're due to inherit!" He shook his head. "You've been so fun to tease all these years. You still are. But it's also gotten, well, just a little bit sad."

There was a loud pounding in my ears. "So Ike's decided you're my new best friend."

"Now you're getting it." He punched me companionably in the shoulder.

I wanted to punch him in the face. "I already figured Ike had some sort of security keeping tabs on the exits. But I wasn't expecting you."

"Always expect the unexpected, Will. It's how you survive." He looked at the table where McKenzie and I had made desperate love, smoothing his hand over the surface. "You have always been a lucky bastard when it comes to women."

"And you will keep your goddamn hands off her," I seethed.

Bran shrugged. "I might. I might not. You know how much I enjoy taking what's yours."

I'd had enough. I grabbed him by the collar and dragged him close so we were nose-to-nose. "You don't get to have *her*."

"That sounds like a challenge. Are we not so sure I can't charm her to my side?" he asked sweetly. "And really, Will. Take your hands off me before my security and yours come bursting in here to do it for you."

With an angry grunt, I let him go.

He straightened his clothes. "You know, when Ike suggested this, I had no idea it would be so much fun!"

"I hate you," I growled.

"I know. That just makes it more entertaining." He straightened my jacket for me then gestured to the door. "If there's nothing else, shall we get back to the girls?"

"She'll never go for you," I stated with absolute confidence. "But I won't have you harassing her."

Bran chuckled. "We'll see."

TWENTY

SWIMMING WITH THE SHARKS

McKenzie

Gwendolyn tried to keep me entertained while Will was gone, but I worried the entire time. What was going on? How did Bran seem to know so much?

When he did return, Will looked flushed and flustered. He looked at the chair next to me then grabbed my arm—not painfully, but firmly—and hauled me to my feet. "We're leaving."

Relief flooded through me. "Thank God," I murmured.

"Don't thank Him yet." He glowered at Bran as the other man sat down.

Bran smiled and slipped an arm around Gwendolyn. "Leaving so soon?"

"Family emergency," Will replied tightly, tucking me into his side.

"Of course. Well, see you Saturday, if not before." Bran gave a little wave.

Gwendolyn gathered up the brochures for the items at the silent auction Bran had won.

"Oh, you won two things in the silent auction," I said to Will. "Do we need to stay to gather them? Or the car?"

He shook his head. "I'll text Mr. Nieves on our way home. Everything can be delivered."

"Okay." I let him walk me out of the hall.

Our driver was already waiting outside at the bottom of the stairs, though I hadn't seen Will text anyone. He held open the back door of the limo for us.

"I'm surprised he knew we were coming," I said.

"I'm not." Will sounded angry.

Once we were in the limo, with the door shut behind us, he buried his face in my shoulder and let out a muffled scream.

"Will?!" I asked, concerned.

He took several deep breaths then dropped the bomb. "Ike has Bran, and God only knows who else, watching us."

"Wait, what?" I could hardly believe what I was hearing.

"Bran even knew when and where we were fucking," he added miserably. "I... didn't want to tell you, but I didn't want to hide it from you, either."

I felt cold down to my toes. "He... what?'

"I'm going to pretend he wasn't watching." He leaned back on the seat and closed his eyes. "Fuck."

"You think he might have been watching?!" I gasped, horrified.

Will sighed. "Like I said, I don't want to lie to you."

A sick feeling washed over me. "And now he wants to see me in a bikini. Gwendolyn said he was going to try to get in my pants, but... this is... a whole other level."

"I just don't want him to pressure you. I know you have no interest, but he's a persistent motherfucker, and he's going to make you *very* uncomfortable." He touched my shoulder. "We could find some excuse to skip Saturday. And the weekend at the lake house."

With a heavy sigh, I shook my head. "No. We're playing nice for Ike and your grandfather. If they're all in on this being besties with Bran thing, then we have to go along with it for now. I just... didn't realize just how trapped we actually were."

"This changes nothing," he responded fiercely. He leaned in close and whispered in my ear. "We're still getting out. It's even more important now than before."

I nodded, my eyes stinging with unexpected tears of frustration. "Sorry," I said, looking around for something to wipe my eyes with.

Will reached into his lapel pocket then must have realized we'd already used his handkerchief.

The partition between us and the driver opened. "Tissues are in the third compartment from the left."

I jumped.

"Thank you," Will said through his teeth.

The partition closed again while Will leaned over me to open the requisite compartment. He pulled out a few tissues and handed them to me.

I wiped my eyes, taking off most of my eyeliner and mascara in the process. "Do you think he heard us?"

"Yes." He sounded so defeated.

I thought of kicking him in the shin again, but I wasn't feeling that great about our situation, either, and there'd been enough hypocrisy for one night. I just laid my head on his shoulder and threaded my fingers through his.

"McKenzie?" he said after a while.

"Yes?" I replied.

"I love you."

I smiled sadly and kissed his cheek, leaving another lipstick mark. "I love you, too."

———

AT LEAST IKE let me pick my own bikini.

Granted, a selection of about twenty had mysteriously appeared in Will's closet—or, rather, our closet—while we were at the benefit.

But it seemed, of the twenty, I was going to be allowed to choose the one I was most comfortable in.

It was creepy that Ike had already known we were going to Bran's pool party on Saturday. I didn't even want to know how he knew my underwear size so well. I was just going to pray it was Polly who'd figured it out.

I chose something modest in a powder blue with, indeed, a matching sarong. It was Will who looked edible in black trunks. I felt a little pre-jealousy. I didn't know how many women were going to be there, but they'd all be able to openly ogle my fiancé. My muscular, well-endowed, handsome fiancé.

The well-endowed part had me frowning at his crotch.

"Problem?" he asked as we zipped around Lake Minnetonka in his blue McLaren convertible.

"You can see it," I grumbled.

Will raised an eyebrow, glancing at me briefly before dragging his eyes back to the road. "See what?"

"You know. Your... thing."

"My... oh for the love... it's a swimsuit, McKenzie. It's hard to hide it in a swimsuit," he replied. His tone held a lot of stress. He was probably even less happy than I was to be going to Bran's pool party.

I felt very foolish. But still jealous, unfortunately. "You can't see anything of mine."

"One, it's a bikini. I already want to gouge Bran's eyes out for looking at you, and we're not even there yet. Two, did you want me to wear a circus tent?" he asked exasperatedly.

I pouted. "Yes."

He glanced at me again then started to laugh. "I can't believe we're fighting over something so stupid."

"It's not stupid!" I insisted. "There will be women there who are going to be looking—"

"And there will be men there who are going to be looking at you. I'm not particularly happy about that," he said.

I paused. "I thought you were just worried about Bran?"

"I'm hoping I only have to be worried about Bran." He raked a hand through his hair, which only made it more sexy. "Ugh. I've never, ever, *ever* been the jealous type. Never. But I don't want anyone to see you in that."

"It was the most modest option!" I protested.

"I'm not saying it's your fault. And I'm not saying it isn't a perfectly good swimsuit. I'm just saying... fuck, I don't know what I'm saying," he said. His hands tightened on the steering wheel.

I carefully put my hand on his knee, feeling like an idiot. "I understand. Trust me, I understand. I wouldn't care if it was anyone else. But because it's you.... Anyway, I get it."

"I just want to turn around, go home, and screw each other's brains out until we can't remember our own names, much less the situation we're in," he sighed. He put a hand over mine. "But I'm glad you're here with me. Even if it does mean I have to watch Bran undress you with his eyes."

"We're a team," I said. "And I'm sorry I brought up the shorts. You're right. There isn't a lot either of us can do about it."

He nodded. "We're a team. We're going to get through this together."

"Maybe we'll have *some* fun?" I hazarded.

"I doubt it. But we can try." He turned down a lane, and then a truly massive mansion came into view.

"Oh," was all I could think to say.

"It's impressive, I'll admit." He pulled into the long driveway, and a man in a crisp white uniform and matching hat walked to the side of the car and opened my door.

I stepped out, grateful to be in flat sandals today.

Will came around the side of the McLaren, handed the valet the keys, then tucked my hand into his arm and walked us to the front door.

A smiling woman who I assumed was the housekeeper welcomed us then showed us the way to the back lawn pool. Well, two pools, side-by-side.

There were about thirty people outside, some at the bar, some lounging in the open pool house. Others were either in or beside the pools.

"One's more of a hot tub." Bran came up behind us and handed Will and I tropical drinks.

"I'm not twenty-one y—" I began automatically then remembered the benefit for Comunidades en Común. "Er… thank you."

"You're so adorable." Bran laughed and wiggled my chin.

Will scowled in displeasure.

"There he is. Mr. Overprotective himself. Oh! Where are my manners? Gwennie! Your friend is here!" Bran called.

Gwendolyn came trotting over from the bar, holding a drink. "Really, Bran. Starting her off with a Long Island Iced Tea? She'll be hammered by the time the burgers are done!"

"Oops," Bran replied unrepentantly, while Will plucked the drink out of my hand.

"Do you… perhaps… have soda?" I asked. I didn't think this was a situation where I wanted to not be in complete control of my faculties.

"Of course he does. Come this way." Gwendolyn looped her arm through mine and took me to the bar, where, blessedly, there was Coca-Cola. Pre-rum.

When we got back, Bran was chortling loudly, and Will looked as though he wanted to strangle him. I quickly went to Will's side. "I've got a Coke."

"Good." Will glared at Bran. "If you don't mind, I think we'll sit by the pool."

"We'll join you," Bran responded.

I had to wonder what it was about Will that made Bran like to needle him so much. Well, he'd advanced to much more than needling now, of course. But it still made no sense to me. Bran was richer. Bran was… objectively handsome. Bran was a successful cog in his family's business and not just window-dressing, which Will had been relegated to. It was just bizarre!

Unless they were doing *actual* dick measuring, I just couldn't figure out why Bran would bother torturing Will this way.

Will escorted me to a chair at a table under a white sun umbrella. He sat next to me in the shade and held my hand on the glass tabletop.

Bran winced at the sunlight on his side of the table and scooted closer to me. We were practically touching shoulders by the time he stopped moving. "There we go. All cozy, and no one has to get burned."

Gwendolyn giggled and moved to the other side of Will.

I knew I didn't need to worry about her. But I was worried about Bran. I was mostly worried about Will putting a fist in Bran's face, especially now that he was trying to look down my bikini top.

"You should go in the pool. It's a hot day, and that one—" he pointed. "—is nice and... cool."

He wanted to see me nip out. I knew it. He knew it.

Will knew it.

"I don't think we're going in the pool today," Will said icily.

"Aw. Pity." Bran grinned at Gwendolyn. "Gwennie and I went in the pool. Before everyone got here."

"Bran!" She let out a scandalized laugh. "They don't need to know what we were doing in the pool."

"They should try it. It's great fun." Bran went back to trying to use X-ray vision on my tits.

"You're not even subtle, are you?" Will muttered.

Bran shrugged. "Why should I be? She's got a nice rack. So does Gwendolyn. Nothing to be ashamed of there. Most of the women here have great tits, but it's hard to find natural ones like McKenzie's and Gwendolyn's. That's the problem with having the money to do whatever you want."

"You don't get to do whatever you want," Will argued.

I put my hand on his knee.

"Most of the time, I do. You've lived that kind of life. I mean, except for the football thing, but that was always a stupid dream. You've already got it all, Will. Enjoy it a little," Bran said.

Will looked as though he was going to snap.

I stood and tugged on his arm. "Let's go in the pool. We came all this way to go to a pool party. It's hot outside, and I think we both need to... cool off."

Will glowered at the smirking Bran.

"Well?" Bran asked. "Did you have something you wanted to say, Will?"

He was trembling with rage, but I subtly rubbed his arm, and he took a deep breath.

"Yes," Will said, looking at me. "Let's go cool off."

TWENTY-ONE
A QUICK DIP

Will

I thought about going straight to the hot tub. I didn't want Bran to have the satisfaction of seeing McKenzie... get cold.

But she brought me straight to the regular pool, and, after dipping a toe in, I decided it was warm enough. I jumped in and held out my arms to her, still grumpy.

Her smile was enough to lift my bad mood, however. She hopped right into my arms, splashing us both. I laughed, and then it was just the two of us again. No one else mattered.

She laid her cheek on my bare chest, and I felt a deep sense of completion. "We should do this in your pool," she said, wrapping her arms around my neck.

I wrapped my arms around her and walked us a little deeper in the pool so I could just barely still stand, letting the water wash over us. There were others in the pool, chatting and drinking, but we were in our own warm little cocoon.

"We should do a lot more in *our* pool," I whispered, and she swatted me.

"Yes, but we're not doing any of that here," she informed me.

"Not in *his* pool, definitely," I agreed. I leaned down and brushed my lips over hers. "This is enough for now."

McKenzie nodded.

Still, it was difficult not to get excited when two assholes came racing by with a volleyball, sending a wave our way, and she had to wrap her legs around my waist to keep from being bowled over.

I swallowed as Mr. Bigshot perked up. Maybe I should have stayed where she could still touch bottom.

"Don't even think about it," she admonished me.

"I can't not think about it. My favorite place is jammed up against its favorite explorer," I groaned softly.

She framed my face with her hands. "Bran."

And just like that, every drop of blood that had been flowing to my penis screamed and ran away. "Can we not talk about him?"

"Wow, that was fast." She looked up at me. "Why do you hate each other so much?"

I grimaced. "So we are going to talk about him."

"I'm just curious. And since it looks like we're going to be spending a lot of time with him, I'd just like to know what I'm dealing with. Or who. Or whatever," she said.

"Right." It wasn't an unreasonable request. "I... well, I guess it started out with some silly schoolboy competitiveness. We attended the same schools, we traveled in the same circles, we basically had the same pool of friends. Then, I don't know. Everything became a competition. Grades. Girls. Sports. Things—such as cars and vacation houses, watches—everything. Who threw the bigger parties. Who invested in the right start-ups. Hell, who hosted the best charity events. It's just something that's become routine between us. Ike must have been laughing his ass off, enlisting Bran to help keep me in line. Asshole."

McKenzie bit her lip. "And did you compete for his girls, too?"

I pressed my lips together, not happy about the direction we were heading in. "I think that's crossing into the territory we're not going to talk about anymore."

"I'll take that as a yes," she sighed.

"Honeybee..." I tried. "Aren't we having a good time? Mostly, anyway?"

She pouted. "Yes."

I nibbled her pouty lip. "Can't we just keep it that way? You know you have nothing and no one to be jealous of."

McKenzie giggled when I began tickling her. "Okay. Okay! Stop, stop! I give up!"

"Good." I kissed her. "Now, can we stop talking about Bran? And other women? Pleeeaaaaase?"

"I love how you include Bran in the same breath as 'other women.' I think you're trying to be insulting," she laughed.

I expressed mock affront. "Honeybee! I would never! That would be unfair to the women!"

She shook with little bursts of giggles. "You're so mean!"

"You're so sweet," I replied, kissing her again.

"You must be insulting me. Nothing else could make you this happy," Bran said, sitting at the side of the pool and dropping his legs in. Gwendolyn sat down beside him and hung on his arm.

I hadn't even seen him move. The man was like an eel! "Get tired under the umbrella?" I asked, not rising to his bait.

"McKenzie makes the water look so nice. And I suppose you're in it, too," he grinned. "So, about your engagement party...."

What fresh hell...? "I haven't even asked her properly yet," I responded with suspicion.

"Oh, right. Ike has that all well in hand." Bran waved dismissively. "Your engagement party's going to be here in the fall. I was going to ask McKenzie if she wanted any sort of theme."

Ike knew how and where I intended to propose to the love of my life?! I didn't even have the ring yet! *Wait... the engagement party's going to be at* this *asshole's house?!* My mind was doing so many gymnastics at that point that I hardly registered what he'd asked McKenzie.

"Theme?" she repeated, staring blankly at Bran.

"Oh, darling, you're overwhelming her. We'll talk about it and have an answer for you by the end of the party," Gwendolyn simpered.

I snapped back to reality. "I think McKenzie and *I* should discuss a theme and get back to you at our conve—"

"No, it's okay." McKenzie interrupted me. "This is something I do now, right? Choose themes for parties?" She whispered in my ear. "Because we're playing nice?"

Right. "I suppose," I muttered.

She smiled at me and turned back to Gwendolyn. "I'd love to hear your ideas. I have no idea what Bran's talking about, but I'm sure you'll educate me."

"Absolutely," Gwendolyn replied. She turned to Bran. "Babe, would you mind terribly if we get in the pool, too? It's soooo hot outside."

"Of course, darling. That's a wonderful idea." He glanced at the drunk assholes staggering their way through a game of volleyball. "Maybe Will would like to play a game with us."

"You want to play volleyball with those knuckleheads?" I asked, glancing at the men.

Bran laughed. "Heavens no. I want to play something else." He slipped into the pool and held out his arms to Gwendolyn, who happily went to him.

Trepidation crept through my veins. "What do you want to play?" I asked.

"Truth or Dare," he said smugly.

Fuuuuuuuuuuuuuuuuuuuuuuck....

"I'm not sure that's really our thing," McKenzie responded, her nails digging into my skin. She liked the idea about as much as I did.

"But it's so fun!" he insisted. "And, besides, aren't we 'playing nice'?"

Gwendolyn looked from Bran to me and back again. "Babe, I don't think they want to play...."

"Of course they do. Don't you, McKenzie?" he smirked. "You could find out a whole lot more about Will...."

"We know quite a bit about each other, but thanks for the offer, Bran," I growled.

"I don't think I'd be comfortable playing with all these strangers around, anyway," McKenzie pointed out.

He nodded slowly, and I thought that was the end of it. Then he snapped his fingers.

From out of the shadows, several servants came melting forward. "Mr. Lockwood?" one asked respectfully.

"Tell everyone else the party's over for today and to come back next Saturday, Marvin," Bran said. "Mr. Masterson, Miss Kent, Miss Evers, and I are going to play a private game."

"Very well, Mr. Lockwood. The master bedroom is completely set up—"

McKenzie tensed, and I held her possessively, glaring at Bran.

Bran laughed. "Not that kind of game, Marvin, but thank you."

"Of course, sir. The bowling alley floors are also freshly-polished." Marvin began listing off the various areas of the house that were all ready for us to play a game. "The boat house is completely stocked. The *Heather* is topped up with gas. Everything is ready, sir."

"Hm. So many options. Well, dismiss the other guests, and we'll give some thought to where we want to play our game," Bran said.

"I think this is a bad idea," McKenzie whispered in my ear.

I nodded in agreement.

Gwendolyn knew we were uncomfortable and bit her lip, but there was nothing she could do. Bran had an idea in his head that he meant to execute, and we were at his mercy.

Marvin wandered off, and the staff began shooing the other guests out. In a matter of minutes, we were alone in the pool area with Bran and Gwendolyn.

"Don't look so excited," he chuckled as McKenzie and I clung fiercely to each other. "I'm not going to eat you. It's just a fun game between friends."

"When were we ever friends?" I asked, frowning.

"No time like the present," he replied easily. "Now then, I've decided this is going to be a drinking game. With shots of Patrón. You either tell the truth or you take a shot. Simple."

"How will you know if we're telling the truth? How will *we* know if *you're* telling the truth?" McKenzie asked.

Bran looked thoughtful. "I've got dossiers ten miles long on both of you. And Gwendolyn, of course. I don't date anyone without it. But you do make a good point. How to make it fair?" He tapped his chin. "I guess you'll just have to trust me."

"About as far as I can throw you," I grunted.

He laughed. "Come now, Will. It's just a game. I'll tell you what. If you can catch me in a lie, I have to do three shots. Deal?"

"Do we have a choice?" I asked.

"Not really." His self-satisfied smile irked me to my core. "I love having this sort of power over you, Will. It's got to be the best gift anyone's ever given me."

"I'll thank Ike properly someday," I returned flatly.

"I know you will. And me as well, no doubt. But today is not that day." He began wading toward the shallow end of the pool. "Come on, everybody out. We have to set up our game."

Gwendolyn gave us a sympathetic wince, probably not knowing at all what she'd signed up for but understanding that it was way beyond anything she'd wanted to be involved with. She followed Bran out of the pool.

"I'm cold all of a sudden," McKenzie whispered, looking a little pale.

"Me, too," I agreed. "Very cold."

"We can't go home, can we?" she asked desperately.

I shook my head. "No. I'm afraid we're stuck."

"Shit." She sighed. "I guess I'm going to be learning about Patrón today."

"No, you won't," I said.

"But I don't want to say some things in front of him!" she protested.

"I'm taking all your shots today. You might be driving the McLaren home. Can you drive a stick?" I asked.

McKenzie snorted. "Farm girl, remember? I can drive anything."

"Good," I replied. "That's good to know. Because we're going to need it."

McKenzie

Ultimately, we settled in the boat house down by the lake. The one that was now 'fully stocked.' True to his word, Bran took out a bottle of Patrón and began lining up shot glasses, five in front of each of us.

Will started to scoop mine his way, but Bran waggled a finger. "Ah-ah-ah, no cheating."

"She won't be doing shots," Will replied with a finality that brooked no argument.

Bran apparently didn't see it that way. "She will be if she lies. Come now, Will. Be a good sport. I know you can be."

"Maybe... this isn't such a good idea, Bran. I'm not sure McKenzie can hold her liquor quite yet," Gwendolyn tried, for which I was grateful.

He shot a glare at her, and she backed off quickly. "No time like the present to learn."

"Of course. No, you're right," she said, pasting on an agreeable smile.

Honestly, I felt bad for her, caught in the middle like this. She had no idea what was going on.

"She's. Not. Doing. Shots." Will crossed his arms over his chest.

Bran mirrored his stance. "She *is* doing shots. Unless you want me to tell Ike you're being... uncooperative."

"You can tell Ike whatever the f—"

I put a hand on Will's arm. "I just won't lie. That's all. It'll be fine."

"This asshole just wants to invade our privacy," he hissed.

"Yes. And isn't it fun?" Bran smirked.

I squeezed Will's muscular forearm. "I won't lie. It's fine. He says he has a dossier on us anyway. He just wants us to confirm stuff out loud that he already knows."

Will glared death at Bran but nodded and pushed my shots back in front of me.

"Excellent. Let the games begin! We'll start with something small, shall we? Truth or shot, McKenzie. Were you dating someone at the same time you got with Will? Be honest now," Bran said.

"I wasn't at the time, no. I'd broken up with my boyfriend before break," I replied. "We weren't really compatible."

"That means he had a small dick, am I right?" Bran chuckled.

I blushed. "That's not the reason we broke up. And anyway, you only get one question at a time."

"Ooh, a penalty on me already? I guess I should take a shot!" Bran knocked the tequila back like it was nothing.

"It's my turn." I thought of turning to Gwendolyn and giving her an easy question. But if Bran was going to make this awkward for everyone, well, two could play at that game. "Bran," I said sweetly, "why are you jealous of Will?"

Bran laughed and put a hand to his chest. "Me? Jealous of *him*?!"

I shrugged. "It's kind of obvious."

"Me. Jealous of him?" he repeated. "Oh, that's rich."

Will just raised an eyebrow at him. "Are you doing a shot, then?"

"I'm not jealous!" Bran snapped.

"Methinks the asshole doth protest too much," Will replied smugly.

"Fuck! Think what you want." Bran downed another shot.

Will smiled at me and bumped his knee against mine under the table.

Go team Masterson-Kent! I thought proudly. Which begged the question, would I be hyphenating my name when we got married?

Bran interrupted my reverie. "It's my turn again." He made it sound like a threat.

"Oh! Do me!" Gwendolyn said, and I could have hugged her.

But he wasn't having it. "I *am* doing you. But you're not getting my question. Not yet. Someone's gotten a bit of a big head and needs to be put in her place."

I straightened in my chair. "Bring it on."

"Are your parents brother and sister?" Bran asked.

Seriously? "One, Will already knows the answer to that one, so if you're trying to shock him, you're out of luck. Two, no they are not. They are *step*-brother-and-sister. They're not related by blood."

Will nodded, completely unfazed.

"Well, that's no fun." Bran stroked his chin, his anger having dissipated into some kind of evil vendetta. "I guess I'll have to try harder next time."

"My turn," I reminded him.

He smirked. "Bring it."

"Why do you *hate* Will?" I asked, rephrasing my previous question.

"Bzz! No, you don't get that one. That's a repeat question I already did a shot for. Now *you* have to take a penalty shot!" Bran crowed.

Will held up his hand. "She asked why you were jealous of me before. Now she's asking why you hate me. Two different things entirely."

Bran rolled his eyes. "Fine, fine." He drank another shot.

"I'm getting the impression he's just not going to answer anything about why he's got a bug up his ass about me," Will said.

"I guess not." I waited patiently for his next question.

Bran eyed me for a moment then turned to Will. "You ever had a better fuck than McKenzie?"

"No," Will said automatically. He didn't even need to think about it.

I was glad he just answered and didn't get riled. I was also glad I was Will's best fuck, but mostly I was glad he hadn't given Bran the adverse reaction he so desired.

"I suppose it would be impossible for me to tell if you were lying," Bran mused. He gave me a wink. "Maybe it's the young pussy that does the trick?"

"It's genuine affection. Try it sometime." Will took my hand under the table. He smiled at Gwendolyn. "You're probably feeling pretty left out."

She swallowed. "Um... sort of?"

"Don't be mean," I whispered in Will's ear.

He nodded and asked, "What's your favorite color?"

"You've got to be shitting me," Bran scoffed.

Gwendolyn smiled with relief. "Sage."

"That's a lovely color," Will complimented her.

"'What's your favorite color'? What is this, a fifth-grade sleepover?" Bran complained.

"So, it's my turn." She turned to me. "McKenzie, did you have a favorite pet on the farm where you grew up?"

Bran rolled his eyes. "I swear to Jesus."

I had to bite the inside of my cheek to keep from laughing. "We had a couple of dogs. My favorite was Trooper. He was a black lab and really derpy."

"Aw, he sounds cute." She frowned slightly at Bran before smoothing her features back out into a placid smile.

Bran didn't miss a thing, however. "What's the disapproving glare about?"

"It's not your turn," Will jumped in immediately. He gave Bran a devilish smile. "Seems you're on your fourth shot now. What happens after five? Game over?"

Sour faced, Bran dumped another shot down his throat. "I suppose it is."

"Good. That means you only have to get caught up in your own assholery one more time, and McKenzie and I can go home." Will kissed my temple.

"Hm. Yes." Bran turned to me. "Well, Miss Know-It-All, can I expect your next question to be for me? And keep in mind, I don't think you can contort that first question of yours any other way. If you do, you're doing a shot."

"Okay." I thought about ignoring Bran this time. But I was fed up to my eyeballs with the way he treated Will—and by extension, me. "Have you... ever seriously injured anyone?"

His eyes bulged. "How could you possibly...?" He turned to Will. "What did you tell her?!"

Will, however, looked as surprised as Bran was. "I never said a word."

"Then what would possess her—never mind. It's a matter of public record, anyway. Yes. When I was your age, I was driving drunk and ended up killing three kids in another car," Bran bit out.

My jaw dropped. "How... how are you not...?"

"You're not in prison either, princess, so I'd keep my mouth shut on the subject if I were you." Then Bran lit up. "And... that was a second question. It wasn't your turn!"

Oh no! I glanced at Will.

He was stiff but still had to shrug. "I'd rather you didn't, McKenzie. But we're playing nice."

I nodded and picked up the tequila shot. "Bottom's up?" I said nervously before pouring it in my mouth.

Immediately, I began choking. The Patrón burned all the way down my throat. I ended up spitting most of it back out onto the table on reflex.

"Rude," Bran said. "And also, now you need to take another. If you can't keep it down, it doesn't count."

"For fuck's sake, Bran!" Will protested, rubbing my back as I coughed.

Gwendolyn went and got a towel, quickly cleaning up the mess. "Maybe we should just count it for toda—"

"Maybe we shouldn't!" Bran snapped.

She scrunched back in her chair and said nothing more about it.

I scowled at Bran but picked up another shot. "To your health."

"Plug your nose," Will whispered.

I took his advice and pinched my nose closed, took a deep breath, and tossed the tequila as far back in my throat as I could before choking it down.

This time, I managed not to spit it out. Barely. But I did cough like my lungs were on fire. It felt like they were!

Bran smiled, satisfied. "Good. I knew you had it in you."

"I'm driving," Will stated, rubbing my back again while everything from my mouth to my stomach burned.

"Good plan," I coughed.

Bran's smile widened. This was not a good sign. "But we're not finished with the game yet."

"So what?" Will asked. "You have one more shot to go, and then we're going home. End of story."

Chuckling, Bran shook his head. "You have five shots in front of you. How much do you want to bet that I can make you drink all five of them before I finish this last one of mine?"

"I'm not betting on that. Drunk driving is not a game. You should know that better than anyone," Will accused.

Bran's expression darkened. "Oh, I know. I do know that, Will. Which is why, if you also got hammered, I'd make you stay here until you sober up. Say, until tomorrow morning?"

Has that been his plan all along?! "Maybe we should just leave now," I said, beginning to stand. I already didn't feel very good.

"Sit," Bran commanded, his tone so harsh I actually did. "Now, we're all going to play my little game. You're going to play my little game until I tell you that you can stop. Do you understand?!"

"You know what? Tell Ike whatever you want. I don't care. I'm not your puppet or your punching bag for whatever teenaged angst you still need to work through, and neither is McKenzie." Will stood this time and helped me up.

Bran got up so forcefully that his chair fell back behind him. "Where do you think you're going?!"

"Home. And you can fuck off." Will guided me out of the boathouse and back up the path toward the mansion.

"If you don't get back here right now, we can't be friends. What will your grandfather think of that?" Bran called after us.

I looked at Will. Will looked at me.

"Guess it's our loss, then," Will yelled back.

We kept walking up the path then through the house.

Then we realized someone had to bring us the McLaren.

We stood outside the mansion like idiots, staring at the driveway as though the car might magically appear.

Bran sauntered up with Gwendolyn in tow, his Cheshire-cat smile giving me the creeps. "Problem?"

Will took out his phone. "Four messages from—you already called Ike?!"

"I texted him. He agreed you should stay here for the night, for appearance's sake. You know how employees' tongues wag. They saw you with the tequila," Bran said.

"I didn't drink any!" Will replied.

"Do those kinds of things really matter? Anyway, I've had one of the guest rooms set up for you both. Maybe later this evening, we can go bowling." He winked at us.

"Seriously, what is your problem?!" I demanded, my stomach roiling. Patrón on an empty stomach was apparently not a good idea.

Bran shrugged. "When Will figures it out, then we'll know, won't we?" He put an arm around Gwendolyn. "Come on, darling. We need to get a head start if we want to have a chance at beating these two at fucking each other's brains out. They get quite loud."

"What?" I gasped.

"Or so I'm told," he amended.

Something told me he'd had it right the first time. Which meant, somehow, he'd watched us or at least listened to us have sex on a different occasion than the Comunidades en Común benefit. We'd been very quiet there.

I felt sick, sicker than I'd ever felt in my life.

"Bran, why don't you go—" Will began angrily.

He didn't get to finish his sentence because I threw up on Bran.

TWENTY-THREE
TRAPPED IN PARADISE

Will

I couldn't have timed it better myself.

While Bran grimaced at his clothes, I pulled McKenzie into my side and touched her cheek. I would have laughed and congratulated her on a job well done if she hadn't looked so sick. "Are you okay?"

"I don't feel good. I want to go home," she replied.

"Bran," Gwendolyn finally said, more firm and less bubble-headed than I'd ever heard her be. "We're going away for a weekend together not three weeks from now. *Please*, just let them go home!"

He stopped pawing at his shirt and glared at her. Then at me. But, thankfully, not at McKenzie. I'd have had to punch him if he did. I'd had more than enough of his bullshit.

"They're staying here. It's non-negotiable." Bran gave Gwendolyn a speculative look. "And you're going to have to watch your tone. How are you going to make it up to me?"

I could see her vacillating, her mind doing gymnastics I understood. Bran was a great catch. Probably the greatest catch she was ever going to land on the circuit. Keeping him a while longer could have her set for life.

On the other hand, I knew she was coming to despise him and wanted to leave just as much as we did.

Ultimately, she chose her future over her present upset. "I don't know, Bran," she simpered, clinging to his arm. "What do you want?"

Bran chuckled. He knew he'd won on all fronts. "We'll discuss that... privately. Some things aren't fit for innocent young ears."

I looked down at McKenzie, who looked woozy. "Tell me where our room is. McKenzie needs to lie down."

"That's better. I'll have Marvin take you. Gwendolyn and I have... matters to discuss." He snapped his fingers.

Marvin popped up like a gopher from a hole. "Mr. Lockwood?" he asked as though he hadn't heard every word.

"Good, you're here." Bran didn't sound surprised. "Please escort Mr. Masterson and Miss Kent to their room. Miss Evers and I will require energy drinks and some Powerbars brought to my suite. Will? Anything for you?"

I ground my teeth. "Miss Kent will require some tea."

"Hangover tea?" Marvin asked without missing a beat.

"Yes. Thank you," I replied.

"This way please, sir," Marvin said.

I carefully picked up McKenzie in my arms. I didn't care if she threw up on me, but I didn't want to make her feel worse.

She groaned and burrowed her face into my neck, snuggling into my bare shoulder.

"Are you sure you won't need Powerbars and energy drinks?" Bran laughed after us.

Without jostling McKenzie too much, I managed to flip him off.

She still whimpered.

"It's okay, honeybee," I said softly. "We'll have you lying down soon." Out of the corner of my eye, I caught sight of Bran grabbing Gwendolyn roughly by the wrist and dragging her off.

I did not envy her. Whatever was about to happen was not going to be pleasant.

My focus, however, needed to be elsewhere. "We're just about there, love."

"Uh-huh." McKenzie panted, her breath tickling my skin.

Marvin finally finished navigating us through the halls of the massive mansion and stopped in front of a solid wood door. "Here you are, sir. Please let me know if you will require anything else."

"Thank you, Marvin. That will be all," I responded and strode quickly into the room. I laid her down on the bed then went to the bathroom and got a warm, soft washcloth to wash away the small amount of residue around her mouth. My brilliant love had managed to get almost everything in her stomach on Bran.

"Is it always like this?" she asked, tossing an arm across her forehead. "People do this for *fun*?!" Then she winced at the volume of her own voice.

I gave a sympathetic laugh. Quietly. "Most people don't start with shots of Patrón."

"Yeah, I can see why." She rubbed her stomach. "Ugh."

I kissed her cute, bare little belly button. "We'll get you through this. Don't worry. And then you never have to drink again."

"I have to," she said.

"Why?" I asked, frowning.

"Champagne. Wedding." She started digging her fingernails into her palm.

I knew what the problem was. I scooped her up again and got her to the bathroom just in time for her to heave the non-existent contents of her empty stomach into the toilet. I gently held back her ponytail. "All right, but just a sip or two."

"What if he wants to do another stupid game?" she said, her head hanging listlessly.

"We're not going to play his games," I replied flatly. "Not anymore."

McKenzie sighed and turned to look at me. "Do we have a choice?"

"There's always a choice, and I've made one. I'm going to see Grandfather myself," I said.

"Didn't Ike already tell you that you had to see him?" she asked.

"Yes." I rubbed her back. "But I'd been planning to put it off as long as possible. I'm going to find out what he wants and begin negotiating. This is ridiculous."

She frowned. "Do you think they did it on purpose? Ike and your grandfather? The whole Bran thing? I mean, knowing what your relationship is and what an ass he is?"

"Hm." I gave that some thought. "You might have something there." The idea made me angry. No, incensed. They already had us by the balls and decided they needed to pile more hardship on just to have a better negotiating position?!

It was a great business move, I had to admit. But a shitty, shitty thing to do to one's own flesh and blood.

"I don't like your grandfather and I haven't even met him yet," she grumbled. "But then, you knew that already."

"And I don't blame you one bit. I've known him my whole life, and I've never liked him much. But now I *hate* him," I said.

"That's his fault. Don't feel bad about that." She sighed. "I think I'm ready to go back to bed."

I nodded. "Probably a good plan." I smoothed a lock of hair away from her face. "Would you like me to carry you again?"

McKenzie held up her arms. "Please?"

Like she was a small child, I lifted my fiancée up in my arms. "This will pass sooner than you think." Where was Marvin with the tea?!

"I hope so," she replied. "Because this is going to get really old, really fast."

I tried not to chuckle but wasn't able to hold it back entirely, my chest shaking.

She swatted me as I laid her back down. "This isn't funny!"

"No, it's not. But your reactions are pretty funny. Not that you're silly, falling-down drunk or anything like that. Just how indignant you are," I smiled, lying down next to her.

"I should be indignant. That asshole tried to poison me!" she complained.

"True enough." I kissed her forehead. "Where is Marvin with that tea? I thought for sure he'd be here already...."

"Maybe hangover tea takes more time to steep or something. Or maybe he's harvesting some special herb from the garden as we speak," she suggested. She caressed my cheek. "Don't get mad at the staff just because Bran is a shithead."

But the staff are watching us as well. I didn't say the thought aloud. I didn't want to upset her more while she was sick. Besides, she was a bright girl. She was going to draw the same conclusion all on her own.

"I know what you're thinking," she said when I didn't answer right away.

"Oh?" I feigned innocence.

McKenzie nodded. "You're thinking the staff are watching us, too."

I winced. "Yes, I am."

"That's still not Marvin's fault. I'm sure he's under orders," she pointed out.

"And being paid quite handsomely for following them," I responded bitterly.

She touched my bare chest, and my dick remembered Bran saying something about Powerbars and energy drinks. "Still, not his fault," she insisted.

I took her hand and kissed it before the warm skin-on-skin contact led to other things. "We'll have to agree to disagree, I think."

"I guess so." But she didn't sound angry about it, which was good.

Then she winced and rubbed her stomach again.

I sat up, deciding to go summon Marvin. "I'll be right back, honeybee. I'm just going to see what's going on with the tea."

"Okay," she agreed, which was a testament to how awful she felt. Usually, she would have wanted me to stay by her side.

I went to the door and turned the handle, ready to give Marvin a piece of my mind.

The handle clicked uselessly.

I turned it again.

Still nothing.

Fuck!

"Will?" McKenzie asked, sitting up on her elbows with a grimace.

"We're locked in," I said.

"What?!" She sat up fully.

"That *motherfucker* locked us in!" I repeated. I slammed my fist against the door. "Bran, you *sonofabitch!*"

Carefully, she slid off the bed and came to my side. She reached out and tried the door handle herself.

I didn't blame her. I would have done the same thing. I would have had to see for myself.

"Oh my God," she murmured, jiggling the handle a few times. "That asshole!"

"That's what I'm saying. Are you a big fan of Marvin's now?" I asked.

She scowled. "No. Not really."

A key turned, and suddenly the door opened. "Did I hear my name?" Marvin asked pleasantly.

I snatched the tea tray from him. "Did Mr. Lockwood tell you to lock us in?"

"Yes, sir. He didn't want you wandering around. He thought you would get yourself into trouble," he replied. It was an easy reply, as though he was strolling through the park and not holding two people captive against their will.

"How kind of him. And you," I shot back.

He shrugged and indicated the large tea tray that I was still holding. "There are two different teas on the tray. One is for Miss Kent. One is for you."

"For me?" I echoed. "Why is there one for me?"

"It seemed only polite, sir. A nice chamomile to calm the nerves," he said.

"I wouldn't need to calm my nerves if Bran wasn't—never mind. Fine. Just fine. You can leave us now," I replied, frowning at him.

"Of course, sir." He nodded to both of us. "Have a nice rest." He left, locking the door behind him.

I made a frustrated sound and set the tray down. There were neat, embossed labels next to each china teapot, one with my name, one with McKenzie's.

"Maybe we should just drink our tea and take a nap," she suggested.

With a sigh, I nodded. It wasn't as though he could poison us, and she needed to feel better. I poured us each our own tea, then shooed her back to the bed, holding her cup while she propped herself up against the pillows.

I handed McKenzie her cup and sat down with mine. "I suppose I should have asked if you wanted milk or sugar."

"Ugh. No. Not with the way my stomach's acting," she said. She sipped her tea slowly.

I sipped mine, then took a small sip. It was the perfect temperature and tasted slightly sweet. All in all, not bad.

"How does yours taste?" I asked her.

"Good." She took another sip. "And it's not poisoned, so there's that."

I groaned. "How is it you always read my mind?"

"It's because we're two smart people stuck in the same situation. We're bound to have the same thoughts," she said.

I chuckled. It really wasn't funny, but then it sort of was.

McKenzie rolled her eyes. "You're doing that laughing-at-stuff-that-isn't-funny thing again."

"If I didn't laugh, I'd probably cry. Or break the tea set," I said.

"Don't do that! It's a lovely tea set," she responded with a grin.

I took a generous drink of my tea. "I'll ask Bran if you can have i—" I stopped, suddenly feeling dizzy. And drowsy.

Very drowsy.

The teacup suddenly slipped from my hand as I slumped backward.

McKenzie cried out.

I only had one last thought.

Bran. You. MOTHERFUCKER.

TWENTY-FOUR
THE EEL

McKenzie

"Will!" I shook his shoulder while both our teas soaked into the bed, completely unnoticed. "Will! Will, wake up!"

He didn't stir.

Panicking, I put my ear to his chest. There was still a steady, strong heartbeat there. I could have died from relief.

"He's fine," a familiar voice said from the doorway.

I snapped my head up only to see Bran in a decadent black silk robe leaning against the doorframe. "What did you do to him?!" I barked.

"You know, you're not like anyone, McKenzie Kent-Killeen. You're absolutely fearless. You don't even realize the position you're in, do you? If you did, you'd understand you're being completely stupid," he said.

"I didn't ask for your opinion. I asked what you did to Will!" I yelled.

He chuckled. "Temper, temper. I guess something in his tea didn't agree with him. He'll be out for a few hours. Plenty of time for you and me to get better acquainted."

"You have a screw loose if you think I'd ever betray Will—and certainly not with you," I snapped. "Now fuck off wherever you came from. I have to make sure Will doesn't choke on his tongue and die because you and your teeny, tiny little... ego... decided to go after things you can't have."

Now he burst out into body-shaking guffaws. "My, you really are a firecracker!"

"Yeah. Yeah, I am. *His* firecracker." I gestured to Will.

"Lucky bastard. But then, he always is." He walked into the room and grabbed me by the wrist, hauling me off the bed.

I screamed and clawed at his hand, kneeing him right in the groin when he let go.

"Fuck, woman, I just want to talk!" he cried.

"We can talk here," I said, heading back to the bed.

He grabbed my shoulder. "We really... can't. Listening ears, you know."

I glanced around the room, wondering if the expensive vase on the table or the well-groomed potted plant in the corner were hiding listening devices. Or maybe the lamp. Or the bed. Who knew? "I'm not leaving Will."

"I promise, I will have staff look after him. What do you think will happen to me if he dies? I like being alive with all my limbs intact, thank you very much," he said.

"Why would I agree to go anywhere with you? What could you possibly have to say?" I scoffed.

Bran tapped his ear, then handed me a folded piece of paper from his robe pocket.

Freedom.

I swallowed. That was one thing I couldn't ignore. If this complete asshat was willing to get Will and me out... that was something I needed to find out more about.

I looked down at Will and stroked his hair off his forehead. "You'll have someone come watch him?"

"Scout's honor," Bran replied.

With a sigh, I stood. I kissed Will's cheek and whispered to him that I'd be back. Then I walked over to Bran. "You had better not be shitting me," I whispered.

He chuckled. I wished I'd just let Will punch him.

Bran led me to a side door then outside and across the lawn to a large guesthouse. I didn't like being alone with him, especially with me in a bikini and him in a robe. I could only hope he was wearing something underneath it.

"We didn't wire this place up because you weren't ever going to be staying here," he explained, unlocking the front door and letting me in. He led me through the foyer to a large living room situated right in the center of the house. A long bank of windows looked out over Lake Minnetonka.

"That's great. Really. Now, you were going to tell me something about Will and me getting out of this shithole we've been thrown into?" I said.

He laughed. "Patience. You would be useless at the negotiating table. There's a rhythm to things. A dance if you will. A courtship. You have to start with compliments and—"

"I give absolutely zero shits, Bran. Tell me what's going on," I insisted.

"We could make it a drinking game." He winked.

"Or, you could lose a testicle," I replied, no longer willing to play his games.

"Ouch! I can see what he sees in you. An edge of danger. It's enticing." He lowered himself into a chair and gestured for me to sit across from him.

As I sat down, I could see he wasn't wearing a stitch of clothing under his robe. Not even boxers.

"Oops," he said, adjusting his robe even though I knew it was no accident.

"The only thing you have to offer that I want," I said, trying to drive the point home, "is an explanation of how you're going to get Will and me free of all this."

Bran grinned. "Yes, of course. But I don't remember saying anything about Will."

I froze. "What?"

"Will isn't part of the bargain. How would I even make that happen? His grandfather would make my life a living hell," he said.

I immediately rose from my chair. "It's been nice talking to you. Thanks for wasting my time. I'm going to go back to Will now."

"Sit, sit. We're only starting the negotiations, remember?" He sat forward, letting his robe dangle open.

And other parts dangle openly.

I was disgusted. "You have no conscience, no honor, and no chance with me. I'm not sitting here to listen to how, if I fuck you, you can get me out of my situation. Any plan that doesn't involve getting Will out as well is nothing I want anything to do with."

"So, you would fuck me if I got Will out as well?" he asked, raising an eyebrow in interest.

I stared at him. "Ex-Excuse me?"

"You would, wouldn't you? You'd spread those creamy farm girl thighs for me and take it like a whore," he said.

"That's... definitely not on the negotiating table," I responded faintly. "You're just... you're just playing. You can't do a damn thing for me and Will."

"Am I? I'm Bran Lockwood the Fifth. Which certainly puts my power above William Masterson the Third *and* William Masterson Sr." He raised his chin proudly. "I can do whatever the fuck I want."

I snorted. "You already said you'll get hellfire rained down on you from Will's grandfather if you try to get him out. I don't believe a word you're saying."

"So Will's grandfather gets a little grumpy with me. I'm sure I've had worse problems. It's annoying, not insurmountable," he said. "Now, would you fuck me if I could get Will and you out?"

A part of me, a desperate part, wanted to jump in with both feet and shout: *Yes!* I would blow him, fuck him, let him do whatever he wanted to me to get Will and me out.

A larger part of me loved Will too much to let another man touch me, no matter what the stakes. Maybe it was the wrong move, but....

"I can't," I replied. "I'm sorry. Whatever you're offering, I won't betray Will to get it."

Bran's eyebrows shot up in disbelief. "You're not serious."

"I am serious. Now, if there's nothing else, I want to get back to Will." I walked stiffly toward the front door.

He grabbed me again as I was walking. "Maybe I'll just take what I want, then. I know you'd be even more delicious willing, especially since it would break Will in two. But this also works for me. I can break your spirit instead."

I fought his grip. "Have you lost your mind?!"

"Like I said, gorgeous. I do what I want." He tried to haul me back to the living room.

I reached back and gouged at his eyes, but he managed to avoid my attacks. Still, it kept him stumbling in the wrong direction, so we ended up in the kitchen instead of the living room.

Bran didn't seem to mind. He slapped me a few times until I felt disoriented then bent me over the kitchen island.

Disoriented or not, however, I still screamed and fought like mad.

"Shut up and enjoy it," he snarled when I stomped on his foot, hitting me again.

I felt him trying to pull down my panties while I struggled. With no other ideas, I reached back and grabbed his balls, twisting so hard I felt something rip.

He screamed and stumbled back. "You bitch!"

Still dizzy, I scrabbled around the island, grabbing drawers and yanking them open. Anything to get in his way.

Bran slammed them shut again. "You are fucking dead. You hear me?! Dead!"

I still managed to keep the island between us, barely. One drawer I opened provided a familiar gleam.

Knives!

I was just reaching in to grab one when he appeared behind me and slammed the drawer on my hand. I yelped.

"You think you're so clever. And strong. And untouchable, don't you? You think that little attitude of yours is going to see you through everything," he whispered harshly in my ear. "I have news for you. It's not going to see you through this."

"FUCK YOU!!!" I shouted, determined to give him as much attitude as I could right up until the end. And I was convinced it was going to be the end once he was done with me. He'd said it himself. He was going to kill me.

Bran tried to pin me against the counter, but I was still fighting too hard. With an exasperated sigh, he let go of the drawer so he could grab my hips. "Stop wriggling, you bitch!"

It was just enough slack. Just enough time.

I grabbed the handle of whatever I could in the knife drawer and slashed out blindly.

He jumped back with a hiss, holding his arm. "I am going to kill you in front of him. I am going to make him *beg* for your life, and then I'm going to take you from him. After I'm done with you...."

I held the knife in front of me. "I've killed someone before. I didn't like it. But you? I think I'd get over it pretty fast."

"You're going to kill me with a paring knife," he snickered.

It took me a minute to focus as there was a terrible ringing in my ears, but what I saw in my hands was indeed a small paring knife. *Whatever. It's sharp!*

"Paring knife or not, it did just fine cutting you a moment ago," I shot back.

His expression soured. "It's going to take a lot more than that to stop me."

I was tired of being on the receiving end of his verbal, and especially physical, abuse. When he reached for me, I swung down with the knife...

... and plunged it right into his chest.

TWENTY-FIVE

BONUS CHAPTER: OVER THERE

Jacey

Caleb and I sat in the back of another nondescript black sedan. It reminded me of the old days, and not in a good way.

"I'm so glad we found you," Attorney General Joy Packard said, looking back at us from the front seat. "If we hadn't, William Masterson Sr. would have been released from prison next month. How awful would that have been?"

"Pretty awful," Caleb replied, barely hiding his sarcasm.

What we'd learned over the years was that there was no end to evil like Masterson's, and the best we could hope for was to shield our daughter from it as best we could.

Mission failed, I thought to myself, sighing in despair.

"So much has happened since you were last in the game. The sheik died, but then so did Ibrahim Abadi, who had taken over the sheik's empire. That was very recent, though. Luckily, your daughter wasn't hurt in the accident," she prattled on.

I sat up in my seat. "What?"

"I'm just—oh! But of course you wouldn't know!" She shook her head. "How silly of me. It's just that so much has happened. I mean, now that Ibrahim Abadi is dead, Interpol doesn't even need you anymore, which means we don't have to try to ship you safely to Europe. It's very problematic. Masterson is kind of a bugger."

Caleb stopped her. "I'm going to need you to rewind to where our daughter was in an accident."

"Well, the two men in front were killed. But Will Masterson and your daughter walked away without a scratch. One of the men just happened to be Abadi. Talk about divine providence. He was just starting to become a real thorn in Interpol's side—" she chatted.

"Ma'am, I don't give a flying fuck about Abadi, Interpol, or William Masterson Sr. What I want to know is where my daughter is, and if she's okay?" Caleb said sharply.

I nodded my agreement, wishing this near-tween of a woman would just stay on point.

"You haven't seen the news?" she sounded confused.

"Does it look like we've seen the news? Since your minion Val picked us up at our cabin, we've been cooped up with no media access." Caleb was angry.

So was I.

"Oh. Right. Well, you probably wouldn't have seen it anyway unless you followed gossip rags and society pages." She shrugged. "But it's been all over social media."

"*What* has?" he asked.

"They're home. They're just fine—living at the Masterson estate. You see, Will and McKenzie are engaged," she said, sounding like a complete fangirl.

"WHAT?!!!" my husband bellowed.

It was so loud that the driver swerved then glared at us in the rearview mirror.

"Jeez! Take a pill. It's really sweet. They're such a cute couple. And, this way, they'll *both* be well-placed to spy on Masterson's operation," she went on eagerly. "Just think what a coup that will be."

I gripped Caleb's hand, feeling sick. "Our poor girl," I whispered.

"They're practically siblings!" His eyes narrowed on her.

Joy laughed. She actually laughed! "That's rich, coming from you two."

"He's eleven years older than she is!" he continued as though she hadn't spoken.

"All right, a bigger age gap than you two, but are you really throwing stones right now?" She arched an eyebrow at him.

Caleb looked at me. "What are you thinking?"

"I'm thinking it's unusual, but as long as she's happy, I won't say anything about it. But I do want to be assured that she's happy. I'm much more worried about her being used as another pawn. Like us," I said quietly.

After a few moments' thought, he nodded. "Yes, that's exactly right, baby. Exactly what you said." He turned to Joy. "We want to see our daughter."

"That's not possible, I'm afraid." She didn't even sound regretful about it. "We can't ever have you all in one place. Masterson would surely do something awful. No, it's better this way. But I will let you watch the livestream of the wedding."

He scowled. "I don't think you understand what I'm saying. We will not testify, not one word, until we've seen our daughter and Will. Not. One. Word."

Her lips turned down in displeasure. "I assure you, you will testify."

"I assure you, we won't," he replied.

"Do you want to go to jail? Be held in contempt of court?" she threatened.

Caleb shrugged. "At least the kids will know where to find us."

"So will Masterson," she said nastily.

"That sounds like a you problem," he responded, folding his arms over his chest. "What are you going to do if Masterson kills us?"

Joy looked thoughtful. "Will is going to have better, more current information anyway. What I'm trying to say is that your safety could very easily go from a me problem to a you problem."

"That's not fair," I blurted, horrified.

"It's the truth. Maybe if your testimony is still enough to keep Masterson in prison, I won't have to use Will or McKenzie. They can go have their fairytale wedding and happy life together without ever being touched by any of this," she said.

"What the fuck are you even talking about?!" Caleb snapped. "Will and McKenzie have already been touched by all of this! Wanted for murdering cops?! Captured by Ibrahim?! Chased by assassins?!"

She waved a hand. "That's all been cleared up. I wouldn't worry about it anymore."

"You wouldn't worry about it anymore," he echoed, incredulous.

"I think she might be insane," I whispered to my husband.

"I think you're right," he murmured back. He slipped an arm around me, and we cuddled as close together as our seat belts would allow.

Joy pulled out a tablet and began scrolling through it. "All right, so you'll be giving testimony next Wednesday—"

"If we see our daughter," Caleb reiterated.

She smacked the tablet down in her lap and glowered at us both. "I thought we went over that."

"I thought you knew we're too old and too tired of this bullshit to give a fuck about your threats," he said.

I smiled. "We're kind of over the whole being dragged from pillar to post thing."

Joy stared at us, her jaw dropping wide open. "You've got to be kidding me. Did I not properly explain the dangers? Hell, you've been in his hands before; you know what Masterson can do!"

"And now our daughter is in his hands. And Will. And we want to be assured they're going to be okay. All you keep doing is talking about how they're going to be so useful to you. Respectfully? Go fuck yourself," Caleb said.

"We want assurances that Will and McKenzie will be taken care of. That you will ensure their safety—and if they want to get out, you will make that happen," I added.

She spluttered. "I most certainly will not! They are invaluable assets! They need to stay right where they are to gather the information we need to really nail Masterson to the wall. Him and his whole operation!"

"For which you will offer Will immunity for whatever crime he may commit under his grandfather's direction. Yes, we've heard the story before." I looked at Caleb. "We're not testifying until our demands are met. That's final."

"You heard my wife," he said.

Joy turned several shades of red, from embarrassment to rage. "You don't have the right to make such demands!"

"Suck it up, buttercup," my husband responded. "You're lucky this is all we're asking after the hell we went through and that you're now allowing our children to go through."

"Will's not your child," she scoffed.

"We can debate the semantics of that all day." He raised that stubborn chin of his that I loved so dearly. "You know our demands. This is a take it or leave it situation."

She threw up her hands, the tablet sliding onto the floor. "Fine! I'll make some calls. I won't promise you anything—"

"I'd rather you didn't. So far, you disgust me, and I wouldn't trust a promise of yours even if it came on a silver platter," Caleb said.

I looked down at the tablet while Joy and my husband had their verbal sparring match. Frowning, I moved away from Caleb so I could scoop the tablet up.

"Who is Bran Lockwood the Fifth?" I asked.

Joy stopped. "What?"

Caleb leaned over me and swiped the screen. "John Anders? Morgan Franz? Joel—"

"Give me that!" She snatched it from me. "You're not supposed to see that! It will taint your testimony."

"Who are those people?" I asked again.

"None of your business. You concentrate on Masterson." She turned to face front and closed whatever we'd been looking at on her tablet, opening a chat. "I'll run your request up the flagpole, but like I said, no promises."

Caleb and I both eyed her with suspicion. "I can promise you we won't be testifying if we don't get what we want," he finally stated.

"Yes, yes, I understood that part." She was practically pouting.

We continued in silence for a while then the driver pulled off the main highway and navigated us to a quaint little neighborhood in Oakdale, Minnesota. It appeared to be an association with town-homes, each as nondescript as the next.

They were attached side-by-side, so there was only one roofmate. I glanced at the home attached to the one we parked in front of and saw a blinking red light reflecting off the glass.

"You might want to let surveillance know we can see them," I said.

"Surveillance?" she replied. "You can see them from across the street?"

"No, our roofmate." I pointed.

Just as Joy and the driver looked at the window, Caleb grabbed me and pinned me down to the seat.

Then the world exploded.

ALSO BY M. FRANCIS HASTINGS

Once Bitten

Submitting to My Stepbrother series

Stranded With My Stepbrother

Snatched With My Stepbrother

Sequestered With My Stepbrother

Subpoenaed With My Stepbrother

Flirting With the Forbidden

Fleeing With the Forbidden

Fighting With the Forbidden (coming soon!)

The Beguiling Baronets series

Deceiving the Duke

Dream Mates

Dream Weaver

Dream Reader

Sign up for my newsletter here: https://subscribepage.io/TfsA3A